Family Week

ALSO BY SARAH MOON

Middletown

Sparrow

Family Week

SARAH MOON

**ALFRED A. KNOPF
NEW YORK**

A Borzoi Book published by Alfred A. Knopf
An imprint of Random House Children's Books
A division of Penguin Random House LLC
1745 Broadway, New York, NY 10019
penguinrandomhouse.com
rhcbooks.com

Text copyright © 2025 by Sarah Moon
Jacket art copyright © 2025 by Ericka Lugo

Penguin Random House values and supports copyright. Copyright fuels creativity, encourages diverse voices, promotes free speech, and creates a vibrant culture. Thank you for buying an authorized edition of this book and for complying with copyright laws by not reproducing, scanning, or distributing any part of it in any form without permission. You are supporting writers and allowing Penguin Random House to continue to publish books for every reader. Please note that no part of this book may be used or reproduced in any manner for the purpose of training artificial intelligence technologies or systems.

Knopf, Borzoi Books, and the colophon are registered trademarks of Penguin Random House LLC.

Library of Congress Cataloging-in-Publication Data
is available upon request.
ISBN 978-0-593-89960-1 (trade) —
ISBN 978-0-593-89961-8 (lib. bdg.) — ISBN 978-0-593-89962-5 (ebook)

The text of this book is set in 12-point Birka LT Pro.
Interior design by Jade Rector

Manufactured in the United States of America
1st Printing

The authorized representative in the EU for product safety and compliance is Penguin Random House Ireland, Morrison Chambers, 32 Nassau Street, Dublin D02 YH68, Ireland, https://eu-contact.penguin.ie.

Random House Children's Books supports the
First Amendment and celebrates the right to read.

For my mother

Saturday

MILO AND LINA WOKE UP AT THE SAME MOMENT, the same way they had the third Saturday in July ever since they could remember: their moms blaring "We Are Family" through every speaker in the house and laughing hysterically at their own joke.

Milo heard Mom singing at the top of her lungs in Lina's room and knew that it would be only seconds until Ma opened his door, practically screaming "Good morning! Let's gooooooo!" as she threw rainbow bead necklaces into his room. They would scatter onto the dictionaries he'd left open on his desk the night before.

Last month, Mom had insisted on going to clean out Gong Gong's house by herself, after his last stay at the last hospital, his sixth in the last year. "I might be the one with the tattoos," Ma said, "but Mom is the tough one. She needs to go clean out your Gong Gong's house by herself. When she gets back, that's when she'll fall apart." Ma was right, of course. The night Mom got back, they ordered food from Mr. Wonton, the place they always ordered from when Gong Gong came to visit, and Mom cried into her broccoli and bean curd. That night, she gave Gong Gong's dictionaries to Milo. One Hunanese-Vietnamese dictionary from 1945, when Gong Gong's family moved to Vietnam, and a 1975 Vietnamese-English dictionary from when Gong Gong and Bà moved to New Hampshire.

Milo was supposed to be working on the translation of *The Phantom Tollbooth,* the book he and Lina had loved as little kids. They were going to make a graphic novel version, Lina doing the pictures and Milo translating each chapter into a different language, but lately he'd just been staying up late with Gong Gong's old dictionaries and avoiding the illustrations Lina dutifully left him. Last night's installment, chapter seven, was buried under the dictionaries. He hadn't even made it past chapter two, and he was leaving for Truegrove in just a few weeks. He pushed it from his mind as he headed into the hall to wait for the bathroom.

"Lina! Hurry up!" Despite the fact that his twin sister always got up later than him, she always managed to sneak into the bathroom seconds before him. It would have been infuriating if it hadn't been somehow kind of impressive. "Grmpphhhh" came Lina's still-asleep answer through the door.

"Lina, I swear to god, you know we have like half a second until Ma's mood goes from 'We Are Family' to 'The Traffic on the Bridge of Doom,' and if I have to endure two hours waiting to get on the Bourne Bridge while Ma fumes and demands silence so that she can 'concentrate' on sitting in traffic, you are dead to me."

"I don't know what you're talking about, Milo. I am a delight behind the wheel," called Ma from her bedroom, coming to the door and raising a single eyebrow at him.

"Totally, ha ha," said Milo as he banged on the door again. "Lina!" he pleaded. The door opened and Lina pushed past him, looking somewhere between zombie and sloth. This was beyond sleepy, even for Lina.

"Whoa. You okay?"

"Yeah. Tired. All yours." She went into her room and closed the door. She wasn't okay, of course. And "tired" didn't cover it. She hadn't slept all night. She sat down on her bed like she was trying to cause it harm—punish it for not doing its job last night. But she knew that it wasn't the fault of twisted sheets or hot pillows. She hadn't slept that night for the same reason she hadn't slept so many nights since New Year's Eve: because she couldn't stop thinking about Avery. But now the day had finally come. For the first time in a year, she would see Avery, and she had no idea what to do. For the moment, the answer was the same as always: do nothing. She sat and stared at the yellow dots on her blue rug until they blurred, then she closed her eyes. Her door flung open. The knob always hit the same spot on her wall, and the gray paint had started to chip.

Mom walked over the tornado of clothes on the floor and sat next to Lina. "Lina, my love, my cherub, heart of my heart, if you don't get your butt out of this bed, I will have to join forces with your brother and kill you right there on the Bourne Bridge while Ma takes her cleansing breaths because there's an iota of traffic—" As if on cue, Ma called up from downstairs.

"Julia! Where are you? Where's Lina?"

"We're coming, Em, promise," Mom said sweetly. She grinned at Lina and nudged her in the ribs. Mom could make Lina smile even when she didn't want to. She couldn't quite muster the strength for an actual smile on this little sleep, but she felt her face warm up a little, and she stood up. "Ma knows that there's never *not* traffic on the bridge, right? If we leave now or in forty-seven minutes, still, there will be traffic."

"She knows. Pack quick—we both know you haven't started yet," Mom said, tossing Lina's duffel onto her bed. Lately, Lina hated all her clothes. Nothing felt quite right. Everything was either too tight or too big or too kiddie. She put on her jean shorts and an oversize black T-shirt and flipped her hair to the side to show off her undercut and the cartilage piercing that her moms had let her get for surviving seventh grade (though she knew it was really a pity present for Milo's imminent departure). She hoped she looked cool and kind of vintage, but her stomach twisted with the fear that she probably just looked like she was *trying* to look cool and kind of vintage. She started shoving her least horrendous clothes into her bag (mostly from off the floor) and threw a pair of flip-flops on top, along with the new bikini she had begged her parents for (though now, thinking about wearing it in front of Avery made her want to vomit). She added a pair of black shorts and another enormous black T-shirt. Maybe that would be her bathing suit this year.

"Lina!" Ma called from downstairs. Lina could see her standing by the front door, tapping the floor with her foot, tapping her watch with her car key.

"Coming!"

Milo was probably already down there with his perfectly packed matching luggage. (What thirteen-year-old asks for luggage for his birthday? Milo, of course. Or maybe any thirteen-year-old about to abandon their entire family for boarding school—matching luggage was probably a requirement for the snobs at Truegrove Academy.) She tried not to look at his room as she dragged herself down the hallway, tried not to imagine how empty it would look in just a few weeks.

The call had come out of nowhere on the last day of school. Milo and Lina had burst through the door with the kind of joy that only a Tuesday in late June can bring, summer stretching out its arms, every drama, injustice, and boring class behind them. It was Lina's last day of seventh grade, Milo's last day of eighth. Yes, they were twins, but Milo had skipped first grade once his kindergarten teacher realized that he was reading full chapter books during naptime and writing them during finger painting. It was weird at first, but they were both used to it now. Lina figured that if they were in the same class, people would still think of her as the less smart twin; this way, most of the time, people just didn't believe they *were* twins, which stung in a different way. But that was other people. When Lina and Milo were together, there was no doubt about their shared—well, everything. They communicated silently; even their moms would refuse to play board games with them because they could cheat without saying a word. They had endless inside jokes that only required a word, phrase, or head nod to crack the other one up. September would mark the first time that they wouldn't be in the same school anymore, but Milo had assured Lina that he'd just be warming Beechwood High School up for her.

They walked in, sweaty and jubilant, throwing their backpacks down with extra force. Ma and Mom were sitting on the couch so they could catch Milo as soon as he arrived. "We need to talk, honey," they said to him. "Alone." They took Milo through the swinging door into the kitchen. Lina tried hard to listen, but they went out to the backyard. Lina wondered, with that kind of little-kid glee that still showed up sometimes, if he was in trouble. It seemed unlikely, but a twin could dream.

Milo was not in trouble. Ma and Mom sat across from him at the picnic table. The same one that Milo and Lina had dripped countless ice pops on between runs through the summer sprinkler. The one where they would cut their birthday cakes in just a few days.

"Milo, this afternoon we got a phone call from Edward Sanchez. Do you know who that is?" Mom started.

Milo shook his head, nervous, and tried to glower at Lina, who was listening from the kitchen window now.

"He's the head of Truegrove Academy," Ma explained.

"Whoa," said Milo. Everyone knew Truegrove, the school on the other side of the state for rich kids and brainiacs (and most definitely rich brainiacs). There were many rumors about Truegrove at Beechwood Middle—everything from the obviously false "sidewalks paved with gold flecks" to the more believable, and enviable: state-of-the-art labs, nationally ranked soccer team, and classes in everything from astrology to zoology. "Why?"

"Well," said Mom, holding Ma's hand, "Mr. Adams

called him about you. He told him about your language skills, your grades, your goalie stats from this year, and—"

"They're offering you a spot for the fall," Ma interrupted.

"Me?"

"Yes, you," Mom said, smiling. "It's not so hard to believe, Milo." Milo looked down. He hated compliments. Compliments about his academics were the worst. Everyone praised him for working hard, but the truth was, it wasn't that hard. He just liked learning, and learning liked him back. His brain built bridges between the imperfect subjunctive in seven different languages all by itself. He couldn't forget the difference between *más* and *mas* if he wanted to. He hated being treated like the prized trick seal at the zoo because of it. But he also hated being bored at school. When his parents told him many years ago, in a conversation not so different from this one, that he would be going straight into second grade, he held tight to their promise: "So you won't be bored." But he *was* bored, and had been for years. He knew he couldn't just keep skipping grades, and so he kept busy, reading his English book in the original French when he was ahead of the assignment. This year, he was finishing the two-year physics sequence at the local community college. On the first day of class, the professor kept calling him Doogie. When he asked Mom and Ma about it, they explained that it was a reference to a TV show about a boy genius who became a doctor at age fourteen, a show that finished airing twenty years before Milo was born. It didn't feel great to have it pointed out that the closest thing to a kid like him was a fictional one from 1989.

"You could play soccer," Mom said gently.

Milo looked up. "Really? They know?" There had been rumbling that the state legislature would take up a bill preventing trans athletes from competing in public school athletics in the next few months. Milo tried not to think about it much; in this purple state, these bills usually didn't make it out of committee. But it would be nice not to worry about it.

"It's private—they make their own rules. And their rule is that you get to be you."

"Isn't it crazy expensive?"

"Not for the kid who would be blocking goals and winning prizes in seven different languages," Mom said, so proud.

"They're offering you a full scholarship," Ma said. Milo looked at their faces. *Joy* wasn't enough. Ebullience mixed with pride and love. Not much room for doubt. Not even for his own.

Ma talked a lot about her grandparents, who had arrived at Ellis Island with not a cent to their name, no English, and a rising tide of antisemitism all around them, not left behind in the old country as they'd hoped. The first thing they'd done after they'd moved off the various couches and floors of the family already in New York was get jobs in a sweatshop and send their kids, Nana and Great-Uncle Max, to school. "Education is everything," Ma said, all the time.

The only person more intense about school than Ma was Mom, though she tried to be low-key about it. But she, in fact, had the smallest amount of chill. Growing up as the only child of the only immigrants, and only

Asians, for miles around in rural New Hampshire had been far from easy, but Mom said it was worth it for the education she'd been able to get. Her parents had sacrificed everything they knew, everything they owned, everyone they loved, to give her the best possible chance at life. Mom tried to use every therapisty muscle in her body to keep Milo and Lina from feeling as indebted to Gong Gong and Bà as she did, but it was impossible not to feel like doing anything short of *everything* would be disrespecting them.

He took a deep breath in.

"You have to let them know by the end of the week, so think about it," Mom said.

"Though clearly there's not a lot to think about," Ma said, offhand. "I mean, this is the chance of a lifetime. They don't have Urdu, Portuguese, pottery, and more college acceptances than you can count at Beechwood High. It's a pretty obvious—"

Mom put her hand on Ma's leg under the table, her *slow down* gesture that she used when Ma started to get going.

"It's your decision, Milo." But Milo knew that the decision had already been made. Who could say no to this? He tried not to look at Lina's face, ear pressed against the window screen.

She beat the story out of him the second he walked through the door, literally attacking him with a couch pillow. "Wow, Milo," she said, her voice higher than he'd ever heard it. "You have to go." She had sounded excited. And so when she told him he had to go, he decided he would. It was unfortunate, Lina thought, that she could do such a good impression of excitement when what she meant was *Dontgodontgodontgo*. But that was a problem for a different day. The problem right now was that Ma's head was about to explode if Lina didn't hurry it up.

Ma was, indeed, standing at the front door. Mom and Milo had wisely already shoved themselves into the car. Ma had the same ticktock expression on her face that she had every time they set out to drive to Provincetown, Massachusetts, from their home in Portland, Maine. You'd think she alone was responsible for getting the entire family to the moon, not four hours down I-95, but her face softened when she saw Lina.

"Come on, my kid."

"You know that the bridge literally always has traffic on it, right? What if we just accepted our fate?"

"What if you accepted your fate as a dead person when we have to sit in three hours of traffic instead of a measly two? We'll stop at Starbucks once we're over the bridge, I promise."

"And I can get whatever sugary, disgusting, not-real drink I want?"

"What the heck," Mom said. "It's Family Week."

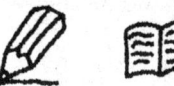

Family Week was kind of like gay Christmas. That's how Lina explained it to her friends at school. It wasn't just a regular beach vacation. Mom canceled her clients and

Ma actually put up an out-of-office message and surgically removed her phone from her hand, and they, along with thousands of other gay families from all over the country, headed out to the smallest, gayest town in the world.

Provincetown was an old Portuguese fishing town at the northern end of Cape Cod, as Milo and Lina had been forced to learn during an interminable tour at the Provincetown Museum one ill-fated rainy Family Week when they were nine. What Provincetown was now was what mattered to them: a town where rainbow flags were as prevalent as telephone wires, where Big-Boned Barbie skated down Commercial Street handing out flyers for her shows, where Ralphie at the West End Salon blared Whitney Houston while dyeing Lina's hair purple the summer she was eight, where the grumpy shopkeeper at the bookstore was never happy to see them but always let them sit down in the aisle and read, where if you rode your bike into town early enough in the morning, the streets filled with the unbeatable smell of ocean and Portuguese muffins. Where no one ever asked if Ma was their mom, with her short hair and full-sleeve tattoos and her worn-out Smith College tee that she seemed to live in the second they got within five miles of Commercial Street.

Even in progressive Portland, Milo and Lina couldn't count the number of times they'd been asked who their "real" mom was, or if Ma was their mom at all—she didn't look like one, after all ("I looked real enough when I was eight months pregnant with twins, my belly practically falling out of my overalls," Ma would mutter). But during Family Week, there were more moms like Ma than Milo and Lina could count. And moms, mas, mamas, daddies, papis, babas, emas, abas, meemas, trans parents, cis parents, nonbinary parents, genderqueer parents, and radical faerie parents and their cis, trans, nonbinary, and everything-in-between kids. For one week, there was nothing special about their special family. Milo wasn't the only trans kid; Lina wasn't the only one with some random hair color. There, anyone who looked at them—even at their worst, like right now, stuck on the Bourne Bridge, with Lina, earbuds in, pretending to be asleep to avoid the blame for the traffic; Milo alternating between glaring at her and glaring out the window; Mom playing an eighteenth round of sudoku on her phone; and Ma, face bright red, trying to keep the rage inside this time—anyone could see they were family.

Five cars behind them on the Bourne Bridge, things weren't feeling so familiar. Avery was sitting in the back of the same car that she had sat in for the last ten Family Weeks, Daddy driving and Papa "navigating" like always, sitting in traffic just like they had for the last ten summers because Daddy didn't see the point in rushing around like crazy people because of "a little traffic." Normally, Avery would have begged for them to leave earlier, waking up at five a.m., bouncing on their bed, screaming "Family Week! Faaaaaaaamily Weeeeeeeeek! This gayby is ready to go!" until Papa got up to make breakfast and Daddy finally gave in to her exuberance. But this year, Daddy had to knock on her door when it was time to go, gingerly, apologetically, the way that he'd taken to doing lately. You wouldn't think that it was possible to say "I'm sorry" with the way you knocked on the door. Avery wouldn't have thought so either, but after this year, she knew that those two quiet knocks were saying exactly that.

"Baby?" His voice was a soft question. "It's time to go get Papa."

Go get Papa. The sentence didn't even make sense, but not much did lately. Since January, Daddy had been staying three nights a week at the house, Papa four. They couldn't even get divorced like a regular family. Instead of Avery moving back and forth between houses, she stayed in her house and they moved back and forth from an apartment they rented in town. She understood, intellectually, why the child psychologist they consulted for their "uncoupling" ("un-family-ing" was more like it, she thought) suggested it. But she probably hadn't mentioned that Avery would be able to hear Papa crying at night, curled against the pillow that still smelled like

Daddy from the night before. She hadn't mentioned that their apartment in town would be the saddest place that Avery would ever go. She'd only been once, so that she could see where they were when they weren't with her: the futon, the kitchen with two plates, and, saddest, the toothbrushes.

At home—or at the place that had always felt like home until six months ago—their toothbrushes had all sat in the same silly Doc McStuffins cup in the bathroom from that one time they let her go to McDonald's when she was five. That Doc McStuffins cup was her prized possession, and even though Daddy thought it "didn't go with our décor," Papa said she could put it wherever she wanted, and where she wanted was in the bathroom, with all their toothbrushes squeezed into it, so they could each look at it twice a day.

The bathroom was immaculate—with the exception of the overstuffed Doc McStuffins cup, it was shining tiles, spotless corners, and the deep tub that felt like a swimming pool. When Avery was little, Papa would perch on the side, letting her swim around until it was time to start the work of detangling her long, curly hair. Papa would run the wide-tooth comb through it, then work in the conditioner, sending her out to the couch when she was done, warm and pajamaed, ready to watch a movie while Daddy sectioned, combed, oiled, and braided. Some lady (okay, many ladies) on the playground would exclaim about Avery's hair from the time she could remember. "What beautiful hair! Did your mommy braid it for you?" And she would say, "No, my daddy did," and point to Daddy sitting on the bench, who waved with a practiced half smile, half-raised eyebrow.

Daddy said he'd learned to braid by watching Aunt Teddy and Aunt Jill get their hair done on Saturday mornings and being so jealous that Grandma Birdy wouldn't braid his. At night, Aunt Teddy would take her hair down and show him how to weave his fingers through, pulling tight but not too tight. Avery took pride in her hair. "Your crown," Daddy always said, "my queen." But lately she'd just been throwing it up into a ponytail five seconds before school. Every time she thought of letting Daddy do her hair again, she thought of when the baby would come, in the new house, Daddy doing *her* hair. This little baby would have this perfect life; all it took to get it was destroying Avery's.

When Papa and Daddy said they were getting divorced, people acted like it was a tragedy for the entire town. Theirs certainly wasn't the only gay family in Montclair, New Jersey, or the only interracial one, or even the only gay, interracial one. But everyone took a certain pride in Daddy and Papa. Daddy was Kevin, a tall, handsome Black man and the head of the oh-so-exclusive Montclair Day School. Papa, or Andrew, was a short, fuzzy bear of a white man ("my polar bear," Daddy used to say) and the rabbi at the Reform synagogue that always flew a rainbow flag and a Black Lives Matter flag. Walking past Temple Beth Tikva made everyone feel like the liberal enclave they'd been promised when they left New York City for a place with yards and houses (but still good bagels and good politics) had been delivered. The divorce was, as Avery's Bubbe had put it more than once, "a true shonda." Avery tried not to think, ever, of the night when they told her (but here's a tip for parents who are getting divorced: try not to do it when it's so close to Christmas—yes, Avery got Hanukkah and Christmas—that for the rest of her life, twinkling lights, Mariah Carey, and the smell of pine would remind her of the end of her family). She told herself that it was fine, that it wasn't the fact that they were getting divorced but *why* they were getting divorced that bothered her. And especially the baby.

On Valentine's Day (again, nice job, dads), Daddy and Papa had taken Avery out for dinner at their favorite sushi spot. They'd been coming here forever—there was even a roll on the menu called the Avery, just a carrot in rice, all Avery would eat when they had brought her here as a toddler. Daddy looked nervous the whole time, and Papa looked like someone had punched him in both his eyes, which was how he looked all the time these days. Dinners with the two of them had become experiments in where the line between painfully awkward and just painful truly lay.

"I have to tell you something, baby," Daddy said.

"Great." No kid loves conversations that start like

that, but Avery had learned in the past few months how much doom could be hiding behind those words.

"Do you remember my friend Jeannette that I told you about? From the conference last year?"

"Yeah, I guess. She's a teacher at Great Lakes or whatever." Avery willed him to stop speaking. In her head, she started reciting the alphabet backward, just as she'd done every time she'd woken up from a nightmare since she was too old to pop right into the space between Papa's and Daddy's sleeping bodies. *Z, y, x, w, v, u, t . . .*

"Right. That's her. Well, there's no easy way to put this, but we've developed . . . feelings . . . for each other." Avery looked up, sharply and briefly, between *m* and *l*. Apparently some nightmares were immune to the powers of the alphabet. "Do you understand what I mean?" Avery wanted to throw her food across the room. She wanted to scream, *I don't understand anything*. She stared at her shoes instead and concentrated on keeping her voice low, nearly a growl.

"You're not gay anymore and you're in love with Jeannette. Great."

"I mean, it's not that I'm not gay anymore—you know, sexuality—"

"Is a spectrum. So my health teachers have told me. Thanks for the life lesson."

"Avery," Papa began softly.

"It's okay—she can be angry."

"You bet I can." She started rubbing the soles of her sneakers against the restaurant floor, tapping slush off them. Sometimes she felt like her anger would propel her clear off the face of the earth. She tapped her shoes against it, a plea to gravity to do its job.

"Yes. Well. She's pregnant."

Gravity failed. Midbite, she got up. She walked out. She stood next to the car while they paid. The freezing February air felt good on her hot face. Every time she closed her eyes, even just to blink, she would see a new house, huge windows looking out on water, warm lights glowing from the inside, and no neighbors for miles around. The lights weren't coming from the chandelier that hung in the front hallway but from the three figures inside the house, glowing with their happiness in each other, their utter completeness. Two figures whose faces she couldn't see but knew immediately were Daddy and Jeannette danced happily with a small baby girl in their arms. When she blinked again, the girl was bigger, Jeannette doing her hair, Daddy reading to her, teaching her to ride a bike. Sleeping in a bedroom that looked like Avery's from when she was seven, except there was no trace of Avery anywhere. Snapping her eyes open, Avery wondered if it was possible to teach herself to never blink again. When Papa and Daddy came out of the restaurant and unlocked the car, she got in wordlessly and went to bed wordlessly, and things had been very, very quiet ever since.

This car ride was just another in a series of quiet, awkward, angry car rides. Avery didn't know why they were going, anyway. What's Family Week when you're not a family? Daddy said, "We're a family no matter what" and "You'll want to see Milo and Lina and Mac—can you imagine if you missed a summer with them?" Papa just said, "We paid for it a year ago, little bear." And left it at that.

A lot could happen in a year.

Avery put in her earbuds and stared out the window. Without looking, she felt in her bag for the lipstick she knew was at the bottom. The black plastic felt smooth and cool in her hand. She rolled it back and forth between her palms. She didn't like lipstick particularly, she didn't ever wear it, but she just had to have it. It was the forty-ninth that she'd stolen since February.

When Mac was little, the ferry to Provincetown was the best part of every summer. Watching Pilgrim Monument come into view over the horizon—the wind rushing past his face, leaving his hair a mess and tossing more than one baseball cap into the ocean—he felt like an adventurer. Mom got him his first pair of binoculars so that he could stand right up next to the railing and look for whales (or dolphins, or seals, or sharks) while the ferry zipped from

Boston to Provincetown. It was usually the best ninety minutes of his year. But this year, Mac was asleep inside his pulled-down hoodie until the ferry docked and Mom had to shake him awake.

"We're here, Mac," she said as she grabbed her backpack and her baseball cap. He'd found Mom even more embarrassing than usual lately, with her hat with the cat ears that she hadn't stopped wearing since the Women's March in 2017, and the way she always shouted "I love you, Mackie-Mac!" whenever she dropped him off anywhere. He'd asked her to please stop, and she always said she would, and she always "forgot." Every summer, Mac and his mom would fly from Madison, Wisconsin, to Boston, spend the night at a hotel, and then take the first ferry over to Provincetown the next morning just for Family Week. He had already informed her that this would be his last year.

"I'm too old for this mommy-and-me stuff, Mom," he said.

"Bad news, buddy, it's basically mommy-and-you

forever around here, Family Week or not." Mac's mom had had Mac by herself, on purpose. "Single mom by choice," she'd say proudly. Carole was a librarian in the local high school. From September to July of every year, she was exactly what you thought of when you thought of a librarian. Sweet, soft-spoken, profoundly nerdy. A knitter. She was one of those teachers who kids believed lived in the school; it was impossible to imagine her outside the library. But once Family Week came around, she shed her cardigan and bifocals for rainbow shirts and sunglasses that she didn't remove until school started again in the fall. If Family Week was a parade, Carole was the grand marshal, the head cheerleader, the biggest, loudest fan. Family Week felt really good for his mom—Mac knew that. For her, it was the one time of year when she felt completely herself. But for him, it was just a different way of feeling weird. Back home, his family didn't feel that different—most of his friends didn't even know his mom was gay; he was just another kid with a single mom. But here, compared with all the various configurations of moms, dads, and every other plural combination in between, it made their small unit feel a little less like a family.

The house didn't help. When the kids had built a block tower together at Drag Queen Story Hour when they were four, their parents all decided it was fate, that they would be friends forever. It was just blocks and storytime at the library, but every summer since, Milo, Lina, and Avery had become his default family, and they'd lived together in the tall, skinny house on the East End. Milo and Lina and their moms were on the third floor, Avery and her dads were on the first, and Mac and his mom were on the second, in the rooms that only had twin beds. Somehow, being sandwiched between the noise of these bigger, louder families underscored the smallness and the quietness of his own. He didn't want a sibling, not really; he had never gone through a phase of begging his mom to bring home another baby or carrying around his Transformers like they were his brothers. If having a sibling was like living with Milo, he was all set, thank you. And one more adult to bother him about homework or living up to his potential didn't seem like a great idea either. But being all in the same house, Mac saw the ease that the other families seemed to have with each other, and he felt guilty that he just wasn't meant to be a kid who made his mom proud.

When he was little, for one week it had felt like they were all one big family, like Mac suddenly had a whole crew of siblings and way more than one parent. He got swept up into their families, subsumed into evenings of highly competitive charades with Julia and Em, practicing for the talent show that had somehow become a tradition with Andrew and Kevin. He hadn't performed for nearly five years—what would he do? When he was really little, he'd play a duet with Kevin, Avery's Daddy, on the piano, but that had stopped being cute years ago, right about the time he stopped practicing.

It felt like everyone had their thing. Milo had his superspy language skills and was generally the most perfect child on the planet. Lina was snarly and cool and could draw anything in two minutes flat. Avery was a freaking model—just looking like her seemed to count as a talent. She was the funniest person he'd ever met, and even though he'd never liked reading, he'd practically memorized the poems she'd sent him over the years, they were that good.

What would Mac do, teach them all how to flunk seventh grade?

"You didn't say anything to any of them, did you?"

"About what?"

"You know about what. School."

"Honey, they're your friends. I'm sure Milo would love to help you with Spanish." Mac contemplated throwing himself into the water just so he would never again have to hear the words "Milo" and "help" in the same sentence.

"Mom! I don't want any help from Mr. Perfect, and I don't want any of them to know. Okay?"

"Okay, okay, sheesh. I'm just saying, everyone struggles from time to time—there's no shame in asking for help."

"This isn't struggling from time to time, it's failing all

of seventh freaking grade." He looked toward the water again.

"Don't judge your insides by someone else's outsides, Mac."

"I don't even know what that means." He watched his mom open her mouth to explain how she meant that you might not know it just from looking at them, but everyone on the planet had their own particular struggle. Milo had a hard life too, yadda yadda, could you imagine leaving home at thirteen? Heading off to Truegrove Academy couldn't be easy. And had Mac seen the latest legislation about trans kids?

Mac would have gladly kicked the butt of any legislator trying to keep Milo out of a bathroom or a classroom, but the truth was that before he could have done that, Milo would have probably written his own legislation, gotten it approved, and been voted the youngest president ever. Poor Milo. Headed to the most exclusive boarding school in the country for free because he was such a supergenius. Truly, Mac's heart broke for him. He spared himself the lecture by slipping his earbuds in and turning the *Assassin's Creed* soundtrack all the way up.

♡

Commercial Street ran the entire length of Provincetown, decked out in rainbow flags and pedestrians who didn't know what a sidewalk was. Cars were considered an unwelcome pest, and tourists took special pleasure in walking as slowly as possible in front of them right down the middle of Commercial. The streets overflowed with shirtless men on bicycles, drag queens on roller skates, the smell of fried seafood, the sweet scent of patchouli from more than one specialty shop, and, of course, straight people who came to gawk. Commercial Street was the beating heart of Provincetown. The house was not on Commercial Street. The house was tucked away on Howland Street, deep in the East End, where it was all art galleries, artisanal tofu, and hushed tones.

Every year, Kevin and Andrew tried to convince Julia and Em that they should try the West End next year—where the shirtless bicycle boys retired at the end of the day and there was always house music coming from someone's backyard—and Julia and Em always said no, they preferred the quiet, maybe they should try nearby Truro next year, they could stay right on the beach and they could always drive into Provincetown for fun, and Kevin and Andrew rolled their eyes while Carole said that she was fine wherever they were, it was just so nice to be together.

The house on Howland wasn't perfect—it was hot, it creaked whenever anyone took a step, and there wasn't a view of the ocean, even though it was just a block away—but for one week each summer, it felt like theirs. Cars parked on the edge of their lawn under the magnolia tree that blossomed each July—parking was awful in Provincetown, and tourists assumed that if they parked on this little patch of grass where the sidewalk ended on Howland Avenue, of all places, no one would notice. But Em delighted in noticing and writing threats of towing (which she would absolutely make good on) on the scraps of paper that she tucked under the intruders' windshield wipers.

Mac and his mom arrived first, and for a few moments, Mac was glad they had come. It was cool and shady in his room on the second floor, with a tree whose branches clicked happily against the window, moved by the ocean air. He shouted a quick "Be right back" to his mom, who was wandering around turning on lights, checking the state of the kitchen like a cat who had to check out every room in the house before settling into the sunlit patch on the floor. He walked down Howland, past the corner store with the best breakfast sandwiches and the playground where he and Milo used to spend hours playing freeze tag, to the alley behind the gallery on the corner of Commercial. An old log sat at the back of the alley. Beyond the log, sand stretched to the ocean. Mac climbed to the top of the log, sat down, dug his feet into the sand, and took his hood down. It felt good to be alone with the sun on his face, smelling the saltwater smell that never made its way to Madison, Wisconsin.

For a few minutes, he didn't think about stupid school or perfect Milo or anything else, just sun, just salt. The air filled him up inside, and he felt like he could float away from all of it. He closed his eyes and could feel his body going up and down with the soft waves that landed at the shore. The sunshine woke up everything from his freckles to the atoms underneath. He felt so alive. And so . . . yes, the word was "happy."

The momentary peace disappeared the second Mac returned to the house, as he'd known it would. He arrived amid a flurry of *hello*s, *oh my goodness, you're so big, I can't believe you're going into eighth grade in the fall*s, kisses and hugs, and *it's so good to be here*s.

Avery narrowed her eyes as her dads greeted everyone with huge, fake smiles, their "Good, we're so good, how are you?" clanging loudly in her ears. Somehow, the biggest news of Montclair, New Jersey, hadn't made it up the coast. Avery slowly shook her head as she realized no one knew what was really going on.

"Hey," she said to Lina, who looked as tired as Papa had lately.

"Oh, um, hey, hi," said Lina. "It's, um, good to see you." They were mercifully interrupted by Milo, who gave Avery a big hug, nearly knocking her down.

"Oh yeah?" said Avery, and for a second it was like they were seven years old again, about to play the Family Week favorite: sock wrestling. Two kids would stand in the middle of the living room, each wearing only one sock. The object of the game was to, by any means necessary, remove the other player's sock. It always came down to Avery and Milo for the final win, and even when they weren't standing with one sock on squinting into each other's eyes, a match always seemed just seconds away. They burst into peals of laughter, yes, because it was funny, and also because laughing felt so good.

"Mac!" Milo called in between laughs. "Get over here!"

Mac came up the porch steps. "How is it that you two are always sock wrestling even when you're not sock wrestling?"

"That, my dear, is the way of the Sock Wrestling Champions of the World," said Avery. Somehow, that made him feel kind of bad, like sock wrestling was one more thing he'd never master, but he knew that wasn't how Avery meant it, so he forced himself to smile.

"Sorry, what was that? Dork Champions of the World?"

Avery grinned and punched him on the shoulder. "Good to see you, Goober."

"You too, Gabber." Goober and Gabber were what Avery and Mac had called each other since they were five. Probably an unconscious attempt to make up for the secret language of being twins that Milo and Lina effortlessly shared.

The adults started staking out their territories: Em and Andrew checking the propane for the grill, Carole showing Kevin and Julia what'd changed in the kitchen since last year. Soon they would all meet on the patio to compile the world's biggest shopping list, and Andrew and Julia would head to the Stop & Shop to fill up three shopping carts full of groceries that would last the nine of them three days, max.

Em poked her head out of the screen door to check on the kids. "While we're getting set up here, why don't you guys go get something to eat? We'll see you back for dinner at six." She handed cash to the twins for all of them and let the door swing closed behind her.

"I would definitely prefer not to be here for the fun-fest of watching your dad fret over how the knives aren't sharp enough and my mom arguing with Kevin about if you can really tell how much propane is in the tank by shaking it," said Lina.

"Well, let's go, then." Avery got up quickly, grabbing Lina's hand and dragging her off the porch. "Gentlemen, attention!" she called to Mac and Milo. "Let's go!"

Even though their fake happy voices sounded like nails on a chalkboard, Avery could see why her dads did it. It felt kind of good to be out of Montclair, where everyone looked at her with pitying eyes, and back with the Family Week crew, who thought nothing had changed. For this afternoon, she would just decide that nothing was weird. She looped her elbow with Lina's and started to skip as they turned onto Commercial.

"Where should we go?" asked Milo.

"You know there's only one answer to that question," said Mac.

"Indeed! Spiritus awaits."

Mac groaned.

"You were the one who said there was one answer!" Lina said, laughing.

"Just because I knew the answer doesn't mean I like the answer! Spiritus is so far away!" The floating feeling had evaporated as quickly as it had come on. Now he didn't feel weightless or happy, he felt hot. And hungry. And not in the mood for a long walk to the same old pizza spot as always. Spiritus was near the West End. The pizza was fine, but the people watching was exceptional. With benches outside, it was the perfect place to sit, eat warm-enough pizza, and watch the town go by. When they were little, nothing was cooler than when their parents had had too much wine at dinner and let them go for ice cream at Spiritus past their bedtimes.

"Listen, Goober, this is tradition. This is what we do." Avery was warming up now. "Gosh darn it, this is who we are! We are the children of homosexuals and we eat pizza. Now where is your spirit-us?"

"That was literally the worst motivational speech in the history of motivational speeches." Mac laughed and groaned at the same time.

"And yet, witness this, you are walking. Thank you for coming to my TED Talk." Milo and Lina applauded.

Rainbow flags flapped over their heads as the kids hopped on and off the brick sidewalks as cars dared to try to squeeze their way down the street. Smelling the salt air, Avery felt like herself for the first time in months. They walked more or less in happy silence all the way to Spiritus, stopping every once in a while to look at a shop that had changed or one that had stayed the same. Lina stopped by the purple shop that had a live snake resting on a mannequin outside to torture Milo, as she always did, his phobia of all reptiles having only increased since childhood. Milo screamed and ran, and they chased after him, hissing between laughs. They raced up the brick steps of Spiritus, placed their orders at the counter, and then headed outside to eat and watch.

Family Week filled the streets of Provincetown with strollers, wagons, trikes, and the occasional child on a leash. The shop owners were not always thrilled by the increase in sticky handprints on their doors, the sippy cups spilled on their floors, the dirty diapers in their restaurant bathrooms, but Provincetown was doing its job: providing paradise for people who couldn't always find it elsewhere. Milo, Lina, Mac, and Avery watched as a red wagon teeming with four little kids rolled by, one asleep, one sniffling post-tantrum tears, one chowing down on a cookie (the possible source of the other's tantrum), and one staring to the sky in a weirdly-contemplative-for-a-four-year-old moment. Their parents alternated between chatting and checking on them as they walked alongside.

"Can you believe that was us?" said Lina.

"I kind of can't believe that's *not* us," said Milo. No one said anything for a few moments.

"I'm not coming after this year," said Mac quietly.

"Me neither," said Avery.

Lina felt her heart tighten. "I mean, I bet we aren't either. Who knows what the supergenius will be up to next summer? Probably interning for the CIA in Beirut or something."

Milo turned red and said, more sadly than Lina expected him to, "I'll still come home for summers, Lina."

Her tight heart softened just a little. "Of course you will! I just meant it's going to be so awesome there!" She put her head on her brother's shoulder. That day in June, when Milo and their moms came in from the picnic table with the News, they all looked at her with worried faces, like she would break in two. When Milo explained he had the chance to attend Truegrove in the fall for free, getting a world-class education three hours away while Lina kept hanging out with the lesser minds of Beechwood Middle, she was determined to seem happy. Thrilled, even. "Milo! This is amazing! Congratulations! Oh my god! So cool! I'm so proud of you!" All smiles and exclamation points. And part of her felt that way, a little bit at least. It was weird, she knew, but she'd never felt jealous of Milo's genius. She had, for as long as she could remember, felt just as proud of it as if it were her own. "That is *my* twin," she would tell kids on the playground, adults at the grocery store, anyone who would listen. She wouldn't let her sadness about Milo leaving ruin his moment, or his future. She had worried that if she seemed anything but Very Excited, Milo would feel guilty and stay home. But in the weeks since the News, it felt like Milo was getting farther and farther away from her. This could be a new adventure for *them,* she told herself, not just for him, where she visited on weekends and they FaceTimed every day after school, where she knew about all of his roommate's family drama and whoever he had a crush on. But instead, it seemed like Milo wanted this for himself. He didn't talk about visiting or FaceTiming, or honestly very much these days. It seemed like he was going to pack up that matching luggage and never come back.

"Avery!" A blond girl stood on the sidewalk, waving wildly.

Lina, Milo, and Mac looked at Avery, who had slipped her sunglasses down over her eyes and was seemingly immersed in her pizza.

"Oh, hey, Maggie," she finally said.

"I can't believe you're here!"

"Yup, here I am." Lina, Milo, and Mac exchanged odd looks, their eyes darting back and forth between this overenthused stranger and the anything-but-enthused Avery.

"Yeah, I know, I just mean, you know, with everything, I wasn't sure you'd come."

"Yup, here I am."

"Are your dads here?"

Where else would they be? Lina's, Milo's, and Mac's eyes asked each other, confused.

"Yup."

"*Both* of them?"

Lina, Milo, and Mac looked away, like they'd accidentally seen the answer on someone else's test. Avery was trying to cover her paper, but the answers were right there in front of them.

"Hi, Maggie. I'm Lina, and this is my brother, Milo, and our friend Mac," Lina interrupted loudly.

"Uh, nice to meet you." Maggie was clearly puzzled as to why this stranger was talking to her, but Lina was determined.

"You too. Where are you staying?" Lina pelted Maggie with questions—what kind of parents did she have, did she have siblings, did she have a donor, a surrogate, a gestational carrier, or was she adopted, did she see the new ice cream shop on Bradford, did she prefer the beach at Herring Cove or Race Point—until Avery got up and went inside "for the bathroom." When it was pretty clear that Avery wasn't coming back, and that Lina's questions would only turn more personal, Maggie said, "Well, um, tell Avery I said bye," and melted back into the crowds of Commercial Street.

When the coast was clear, Avery emerged. "Thanks," she said. "Let's go."

"You got it," Lina replied.

"That was weird," said Mac.

"We need fudge" was Avery's only reply.

They walked through the blue barn that housed small

shops and stalls that changed each year. They went into the candy shop, crowded as it would be all week with tiny, whiny, screaming people, and reached over their heads to procure saltwater taffy, fudge, and two giant M&M cookies. Then they headed to the back, where the patio led down to the water.

"Gabber," said Mac between bites of cookie, "you know you're going to have to tell us what the hell she was talking about, right?"

"Yeah," said Avery, mouth full. "But don't make me ruin my fudge. And please god, don't tell your moms."

After the fudge, cookies, and taffy were reduced to crumbs and wrappers, they started walking down the beach. It ran along the entirety of Commercial Street along the backs of restaurants and bars, inns and houses. Technically—okay, definitely—it was private property, and some folks certainly looked up surprised from their grills or their outdoor showers when the four of them waltzed through their backyards. None of the kids would have been bold enough to straight-up trespass on their own, but together, it didn't feel illegal or even rude. It felt like these were their beaches, their backyards—like together, just for this week, they could do anything.

They stopped when they got to the Angel Foods market on the East End. There were logs set out on the beach behind the market for hungry customers, and Mac and Milo plopped down, declaring a break.

"So?" said Mac, looking expectantly at Avery.

"They're splitting up," said Avery flatly.

"Whoa," said Milo. "Kevin and Andrew, the world's most charming couple?"

"Yeah, I guess not so charming anymore. Everyone at home knows; it's been a whole thing. It's like they destroyed the town mascot or something."

"You okay?" asked Lina.

"I mean, not really. And then there's the baby."

Three heads couldn't have whipped around faster.

"What baby?" they asked in unison.

"Well, Kevin apparently likes the ladies now. He fell for some teacher at a conference, Jeannette, and decided that if he was going to destroy our family, he might as well get himself a fancy new straight one, so she's knocked up and I'm getting a baby sister. So. There's that."

"Whoa," said Mac, unsure of what else to say. The twins said nothing, their jaws dropped.

"Yup," said Avery.

The cold quiet that had been following her since February rushed against her skin like it was blowing up from the ocean. She tried not to blink, but there they were again, the three happy figures, the big house, not even a faint trace of Avery. She opened her eyes.

"Who wants a seltzer? Just me? Okay."

She stood up, brushed off her shorts, and headed into the market. Inside Angel Foods, fans blew in every direction and a breeze came through the screen doors, but the air was always warm. Avery had done this so many times since February, but never here in Provincetown.

Angel Foods was the first place she'd ever ridden her bike to alone. She and her dads used to sit out on those logs in the middle of a hot afternoon, buy a box of ice pops, and eat as many as they could before they all melted. Then, sticky and a little dizzy from the sugar, they'd walk their bikes home for dinner.

It was too hot in here. She headed to the seltzer case, letting her hands trail across the cool glass. She picked her favorite, grapefruit, and went to the register to pay. There were no lipsticks at Angel Foods; a lip balm would have to do. They were right by the register. She handed over a ten, and when the cashier went to make change, she slid the thin yellow tube into her pocket silently. Lina watched from the doorway.

Sunday

LINA ROLLED OUT OF BED AS THOUGHTS OF YES-terday rolled in. Things had been so normal with Avery; she had even held her hand. Avery had seemed happy to see her. Maybe that was her way of telling Lina that she'd read the letter?

Last winter—the winter of her discontent, Mom constantly joked—Lina had spent all of the holiday break watching *Grey's Anatomy* and playing *Animal Crossing*. After three days, Mom suggested she take a shower. After four days, Ma demanded it and then bribed her with the promise of making her favorite comfort food, matzoh ball soup. The balls were perfect, fluffy the way Nana, Ma's mom, had made them. ("You remember this," she would say every Passover as Lina held the bowls and Nana ladled the soup. "It's the seltzer. Seltzer makes them fluffy. Water? Hard as rocks.") But the matzoh balls turned cold and gelatinous as another episode played, and then another.

Ma had come into her room, where the only light was the glow of her computer screen. She slammed Lina's laptop closed and turned on the lights.

"Kid, you've got it bad," she said, taking the cold soup from Lina before sitting on her bed.

"Got what?" asked Lina, annoyed that Ma had closed her computer right as Meredith Grey was about to face yet another life-altering crisis.

"Oh, what, playing dumb now? You think I don't

know what lovesick looks like? I won't make you tell me about it, but I will tell you this: whoever they are, they'd be lucky to have you."

Lina rolled over and put her head into the pillow, covering her ears.

"I know, I know. But I'm right. Anyway, you should probably say something to them. This part right here is the worst part, and you're running out of *Grey's*."

"I will never run out of *Grey's*," Lina said. And she was right. But nonetheless, Lina decided that before she could start season thirteen, she had to bite the bullet. And that's exactly what it felt like—a bullet that could shatter everything.

> Dear Avery,
>
> I don't think I've ever written a letter before, except for maybe thank-you notes before my moms gave up on forcing us to write those. Ha ha. God, this is awkward.
>
> I guess I wanted to say that I miss you. It's

weird—I can imagine you sitting here. You'd look at me with that look like, Get on with it. So I'll try to. I like you. There. That's it. That's the whole point of this whole dumb letter. I like you. You're pretty. I miss you. Is this the part where I include boxes for you to check yes or no if you like me too? Nah. You'll tell me. Or, please, let's pretend I never sent this.

Love (is that weird now?),
Lina

Avery never wrote back. Every morning since then, Lina'd woken up with the last line repeating in her head: *You'll tell me. Or, please, let's pretend I never sent this.* Avery hadn't spoken to her at all until yesterday, and still, all they'd talked about was pizza and divorce. On good days, Lina let herself believe that the letter had gotten lost in the mail and never arrived. On bad days, she figured that Avery was doing exactly what she'd asked, pretending she'd never sent it.

She looked over to Milo's empty bed—Family Week was the one time a year when they still shared a room like little kids. Where was he? Her door burst open.

"Is your nose broken?" asked Avery as she barged in.

"Huh?" Lina brought her hands to her nose, covering her cheeks, which had turned warm and red as soon as she heard Avery's voice.

"Earth to Lina! There are pancakes in the kitchen. The whole house smells like them. Come on!" Avery grabbed her hand, and Lina tried to ignore the sparks of electricity that flew up her arm as they ran downstairs.

Downstairs, things were as they always were, and also not quite. Sunlight poured onto the ugly brick-red tiles with the faded perma-dirty grout, making them seem to glow from the inside like gems. Kevin and Em sipped coffee in silence on the porch, the screen door carrying in the sound of crickets and grass growing in the heat. Avery glanced their way, wondering how long Daddy could keep up the normal act before Em caught on. Milo stood at the stove. With Milo, even pancakes seemed like a new language he was quickly learning, following each step, ladling with a careful eye.

"You made breakfast?" Avery asked hungrily.

"Sure," said Milo with a shrug.

"I'll take five," said Avery.

"Put some chocolate chips in mine," said Lina.

"Lina, you don't think that after thirteen years I know how you like your pancakes? The chocolate chip, slightly burned, yet still soggy in the middle pancakes are on the red plate that you like."

"He loves me, he really loves me." Lina pretended to throw herself at Milo's feet. She hugged his legs just a little extra tight, happy that even though he seemed so far away lately, he still knew how to make her a pancake.

On the other side of the counter, Carole poured herself a cup of tea. "It's so lovely of you to do this, Milo. So responsible."

"It's not a problem. I like cooking." The tips of Milo's ears turned red, the way they always did when he was embarrassed. Milo wasn't making pancakes to be responsible, he was making them because he couldn't sleep last night, but he didn't say that. He couldn't, not when Truegrove was supposed to be some miraculous dream come true, according to everyone. Everyone but him. He had hoped that at Family Week, the threat of Truegrove would fade, but instead it woke him up at five a.m., and only the sizzling of pancakes could quiet his brain.

Just then, Mac blew through the kitchen, skateboard in hand.

"Mac, did you see these amazing pancakes that Milo—" But Mac was already out the door, the *chunk-chunk-chunk* of his wheels on the pavement growing more distant every second. Carole gave a *What did I say?* shrug and walked out onto the porch to join Kevin and Em, staring after Mac but saying nothing.

Mac loved pancakes. He loved the crisp edges and the hot middles; he loved the way syrup pooled on the plate and swirled with the butter. Mac didn't know that the smell of pancakes could make him feel so mad. But lately, okay, not lately, for his entire freaking *life,* Milo had just been so perfect. Perfect tests, perfect brain, perfect son. And Mom couldn't get enough. *Mac, did you see his pancakes? Mac, why don't you have Milo tutor you? Mac, did you know that Milo got a free ride to the fanciest school on the planet while you failed seventh grade? Mac, did you see Milo randomly cooking breakfast for nine people and being the perfect child?*

Mac swerved around cars, on and off the curb, with what he knew was dangerous speed. He finally came to a stop in front of the Portuguese Bakery and ordered the biggest malassada he could find, telling himself it was so much better than Milo's pancakes anyway. It was hot from the fryer, just the right mix of crisp and fluffy.

☆ ✏️ ⛵

"Get your binoculars ready, party people—it's whale-watching day!" Carole yelled from the porch to the kitchen, as if everyone didn't know. Family Week had a certain rhythm to it, and everyone knew that Sunday morning was reserved for the whale watch Carole insisted they go on.

"Whales wait for no one," cheered Andrew.

"His weird, happy act is kind of creepy," Avery whispered to Lina as they walked out.

"You're sure they haven't told the moms?"

"Totally. I think they're trying to see how much they can get away with before it comes out."

Lina thought about Avery slipping the lip balm into her pocket yesterday. Maybe everyone was trying to get away with something.

"Okay, happiest campers, we're here," said Avery to Carole and Papa, rolling her eyes.

"Great," said Julia as she came down the stairs. "We're just missing Mac. Have you all seen him?"

"Yeah, I can—" Milo started to volunteer.

"No, I'll go." Avery slipped out of the house before anyone could offer to go with her.

Avery knew that Mac was always kind of grumpy, but he seemed plain mad this year. And if anyone could get the Goober to calm down, it was Avery. She walked to the log in the alleyway, and there he was, headphones on, sugar from the malassada all over his lap.

"GOOBER!" She lifted up a headphone and shouted directly into his ear. He jumped a foot into the air.

Mac screamed, then laughed. "You're insane."

"And that is why you love me. Now pay attention. We share that house with THREE, count 'em, THREE lesbian mothers. If you don't want to be subject to a trifecta of lesbian emotional grilling, you need to wipe off your pants, get out whatever bug crawled up your butt this morning, and come back to the house ready to whale watch."

"Uggggghhhhh," groaned Mac. Not the whales again. The year he was seven, he had been obsessed with them. He and his mom had driven all the way to Milwaukee every weekend for a year just to go to the aquarium. They didn't have whales, of course—maybe that was why Mac became so interested in them. Knowing he couldn't see one made them all the more exciting. That summer, they went on a whale watch, keeping an eye out for the sharks that dotted Cape Cod waters as much as for the whales themselves, and Milo had been just as excited as Mac. They'd built Lego whales and read whale books, but then Milo started learning the words for whale (and baleen, and blowhole, and rostrum, and dorsal ridge) in as many languages as he could. And then Mac lost all interest, or at least interest in ever talking about it with Milo, Carole, or anyone else ever again.

"Carole is gonna Carole, and we are gonna whale watch. Those are the facts, my friend. Now move." Avery pulled him to his feet.

It started with Googling all the words for a dorsal ridge in different languages, and then asking to learn a language even though school didn't start teaching them until fourth grade. Mom insisted on Hunanese first. He had to do a year of Hunanese lessons before he was allowed to start with the rest of the languages. She'd laughed, "Listen, you will get lots of chances for freedom and self-expression. This just isn't one of them." It wasn't very like her; Ma was usually the one with the thoughts about the Way Things Must Be Done. And so Milo did the lessons, and he'd liked them, and he'd liked the tones and the characters and the fact that Gong Gong's face lit up when, after a few months, Milo could tell him about his day, or ask about the adventures of Fluffy, his ancient, angry cat, in the same language that Gong Gong's parents had spoken to him.

Gong Gong had always been tentative with Milo, like he was afraid he would break him by messing up his pronouns, or make Mom mad if he asked the wrong question. He was respectful, but distant, in English. But in Hunanese, the ice that had always stretched out between them cracked in seconds, and Milo could feel Gong Gong closer than ever.

When they were eight, Milo and Mac had nearly come to blows over whether a picture in a book was a beluga or an orca, and that was it for their whale enthusiasm. Milo had gotten Hunanese and Gong Gong out of it, and Mac didn't have to talk to Milo about whales anymore. But their parents had already signed them up for Whale Camp at the Center for Coastal Studies, and so they went. Each day of Family Week, year after year, Milo and Mac would head off to listen to experts argue about orcas and beluga whales and meet with the team that worked on disentangling the whales and turtles that got stuck in fishing gear.

It wasn't so bad, and Mac liked the turtles, though he dared not say anything for fear that he would be immediately shipped off to Turtle Camp—that's how desperate it seemed like his mom was for him to "find a passion." Which is why, every single year, they all marched down the pier to board the boat for a whale watch—"Mac's passion"—like it or not.

Lina had come to the conclusion that, in fact, no one liked the whale watch. But she wasn't going to be the one to say so, not today, when everything already felt weird. So she pretended. She pretended to be fascinated by the guide who shouted into a bullhorn at the front of the ship about environmental responsibility and the possibility of glimpsing a dolphin today. She pretended not to notice that when Avery came up from going to the bathroom, she had a new lump in her pocket the size of a Life Savers roll. And then she pretended not to be completely grossed out when Milo started puking his guts out over the side.

"Lob-ster! Lob-ster! Lob-ster!" Lina shouted as they disembarked. Carole laughed and put her arm around Lina's shoulders, joining in. "Lob-ster! Lob-ster!" Every year after the whale watch, they went to dinner at the lobster shack. The best parts of Family Week were the traditions, big and small, that linked them to each other one year to the next. With the fall threatening to take Milo away from her for what felt like forever, Lina was more excited than usual for the ritual consumption of massive amounts of seafood that awaited them. Mac was looking forward to the three-pound lobster he would order, the hot corn, the butter melting down the sides. What was it about spending the day on the ocean admiring the living creatures that created a thriving ecosystem for all of us that made you want to eat them? Why was that okay? Avery asked these and other questions that the adults didn't seem to hear, or know how to answer, as they stood in line at the seafood shack.

"Why don't you go get us a table?" Daddy finally said to her, quietly still but more firm than he had sounded in months. She stomped off, taking Lina, Milo, and Mac with her. Like sharks circling, they waited for the family that was sitting at their favorite picnic table, the one closest to the water, to leave. When they finally did, the kids staked their claim immediately, not even letting the dad come back to wipe down the table.

"Don't worry," Milo said with a charming grin, "I'm happy to take care of it." He plucked the napkin from the stranger's hand and started to clean.

"Nicely done," Avery said, giving Milo a high five.

♡

It was funny how silence could go from easy to awkward. When Lina, Milo, Mac, and Avery were at the picnic table, they were quiet but happy. They watched the tide coming in, remembering being little kids running barefoot into the water before dinner, the sounds of their parents laughing at the picnic table behind them. When Em and Andrew appeared with the food, and Julia, Kevin, and Carole came next with drinks, things stayed just as quiet, but the air felt different, heavier, breakable. When everyone was seated, Carole lifted her glass. "Cheers, queers," she said, and they all clinked plastic cups of lemonade.

"Here's to the last Family Week," Mac mumbled. Avery elbowed him in the ribs.

"Knock it off," she hissed. "The role of angsty teen has already been filled by me."

"What was that, Mac?" asked the grown-ups a few seats down the table. Avery elbowed him again and gave him a sharp nod.

"Oh, nothing," he said. "I just said 'Here's to Family Week.'"

"Hear, hear!" Kevin and Andrew exclaimed with irritating zeal.

"Happy now?"

"No, but let them be. It's fine. We'll ruin their hopes and dreams another night, okay? I promise."

♡

After dinner, they stood at the other side of the lobster shack, which sold ice cream. The long list of flavors provided merciful relief from the quiet. There were questions of Moose Tracks versus Cookie Dough and why anyone would get sorbet, and an unexpected defense of sorbet from Mac, and pretty soon they were ordering, then sitting on the beach for their usual after-dinner game of charades.

Em went first, acting out a movie she had never seen but vaguely knew was about drag queens. The kids hadn't seen it either, or any movie with an eight-word title, for that matter, but watching Em pretend to paint her face, don heels, shake her boobs, and prance around the beach was worth it no matter what. Julia and Carole shouted ridiculous guesses into the night air: *"Mrs. Doubtfire the Butch Lesbian Drag Queen!"* *"We're All Born Naked and the Rest Is Drag!"* It was Kevin and Andrew who shouted *"To Wong Foo, Thanks for Everything! Julie Newmar"* in complete sync. Julia, Em, and Carole all laughed and joked about how two people who were so in love should never be allowed on the same team. Avery looked away. Lina tried to grab for her hand to squeeze it, to say, *I see you,* but Avery crossed her arms over her chest. Andrew smiled, clenching sand between his fingers like a stress ball, and Kevin said, "Oh man, I am beat," faking a yawn. Just like that, the game was over. Just like that, stony silence settled right on top of all of them.

Monday

"MILO! MAC! WHALE CAMP!"

It was possibly the worst way anyone has ever been woken up. Mac rolled out of bed, grumbled loudly so his mom would know he was up, and got dressed. Milo was already downstairs, frothing milk for the grown-ups' coffees.

Mac couldn't have rolled his eyes harder. "Let's go."

Now that they were thirteen, Mac and Milo could work at Whale Camp as counselors in training. When they got to the Center for Coastal Studies (which everyone just called CCS), the director, Joe, tossed them their blue uniform T-shirts and hats and pointed them in the direction of a very, very loud group of six-year-olds.

Milo plopped down, and almost like magic, the six-year-olds all turned their attention to him.

"Well, hi, everyone! Let's go around and say our names and our favorite sea creature." It was like he'd been corralling groups of wily six-year-olds for years. Just one more natural gift. Mac scowled and stood around the back, checking off names on the clipboard. It was going to be a long week.

Lina and Avery always went to the Family Week camps. Each day, there were workshops for all the kids, run by kids of queer parents who had grown up and now wanted to be of service to other gaybies. Avery and Lina usually went to workshops together, but Lina wasn't sure what Avery would want to do this year. She wasn't sure of anything when it came to Avery.

"What are you going to?" Avery asked as they walked toward town.

"I'm thinking the zine workshop," said Lina, non-committal. She wanted to be able to change her mind depending on what Avery was going to do.

"Same."

"Cool."

"Cool."

Avery cast a quick glance at Lina, whose undercut showed off her new piercing.

"I like your haircut."

"Thanks." Lina looked over at Avery as quickly as she could, terrified that she would accidentally stare at her. Avery had woken up early to wash her hair, and it hung in beautiful, dark curls that seemed to go on forever. Lina wanted to smell it, and then she wanted to punch herself in the face for being a creep.

The zine workshop was on the top floor of the library, the same room where they had first met as four-year-olds nearly a decade ago. At the front of the room, around a big conference table with art supplies, magazines, scissors, glue, and a speaker on it, were other teenagers and what looked like two college kids.

"Hi, everyone, I'm Alia. I use she/her pronouns." Alia was tall, with locs piled on top of her head, tied up with a bright yellow scarf. She had enormous black-framed glasses and a black tattoo of a panther that moved when she gestured to her cohost. Avery and Lina exchanged a glance that meant one thing: Alia was maybe the coolest person they'd ever seen.

"And I'm Simon. I use he or they pronouns. Nice to meet you guys! We're really excited to get going. Who knows what a zine is?"

If Alia was the coolest person in the world, Simon was a good contender for runner-up. Simon was wearing a black Bikini Kill T-shirt and had two long black braids. Lina wondered if he was Asian, maybe mixed like her. Simon passed out a bunch of stapled-together papers, soft and worn with time and reading. They looked kind of like homemade magazines, but not the kind that Avery's dads brought home as guilty pleasures from time to time with news about a fallen starlet or a scandal about the child of a former president. They had titles like *shortandqueer* and *Blasian Women I Look Up To,* and when Avery and Lina held them, they could feel the hands that had held them before in a way that was totally different from, say, a library book. It was as if by holding them in their hands, they'd entered a club with the people who'd found themselves on these photocopied, stapled pages before them.

"Zines can be whatever you want them to be. Hey, Simon, have you ever made a zine?" Alia asked with a smile, obviously knowing the answer.

"Why, yes, I have, Alia, thank you for asking!" They giggled at their own silliness. "I've made zines on all sorts of things—from Stop Asian Hate to a guide to the best snacks at Trader Joe's. People, Trader Joe's mochi snacks. I brought seven bags of them for Family Week. I'll share if you're a good group."

"Mochi snacks should be the official snack of Family Week," said Alia. The chemistry between them was hard to nail down. Were they friends? Something more? Whatever they were, it was a whole lot of fun to watch. "Anyway, y'all, these can be whatever you want them to be. While there's a longer history of them, the kind of zines that we're going to focus on are the kind that started during the Riot Grrrl movement of the early nineties. Now, who knows what a Riot Grrrl is?"

Simon reached for the speaker, and everyone spent the rest of the afternoon blaring a retrospective of Riot Grrrl music, from Bikini Kill (hence Simon's T-shirt) and Sleater-Kinney all the way up to Big Joanie and the Linda Lindas, while cutting out pictures and drawing and stapling and scribbling down poems, lists of favorite foods, and secrets.

"Here's the thing, Simon," Alia said as they were wrapping up.

"What's that, Alia?" Their schtick still hadn't lost its charm.

"My zine is about marshmallows, and that's not very important. Maybe I should throw it in the trash." She dramatically dangled her pages over the recycling bin.

"Nooooooo!" screamed Simon, kicking the recycling bin across the room, surprising themself with their own strength as scraps of paper flew everywhere. "Oops, well, never you mind. Listen, Alia, your voice is important, even if what you're talking about isn't. And for the record, I think that marshmallows are important. There's so much to consider: Peeps? S'mores? Can you make a decent vegan marshmallow? What proportion of Rice Krispies to marshmallow is the true golden rule? Regardless, it's not the topic, it's the practice." He turned to the group now. "You have to practice using your voice, so that when it matters, you know where to find it. See you sweet people tomorrow." Across the table from Lina, a girl with curly brown hair and green eyes caught her eye and smiled. Lina forgot how to put her backpack on, twisted the straps, took it back off, put it back on, and ran to meet up with Avery.

Over at the CCS, things weren't nearly as inspirational. At the end of the day, after cleaning up one pee accident and countless juice spills, bandaging an invisible wound, and separating Jack R. from Jack F. at least seventeen times, Mac was not exactly thrilled to do it all again the next day.

Milo, on the other hand, seemed to be having the time of his life. Kids flocked to him, the older counselors were already giving him bigger responsibilities (that coincidentally seemed to relieve him of the juice- and pee-cleaning kind), and he was starting to plan some overly complicated scavenger hunt for the kids tomorrow.

At the staff meeting, Joe said that he had bad news. "Listen, everyone, I appreciate your efforts today, and you're all doing a great job. Unfortunately, one of our disentangling team interns is out this week. We really need some help. If any of you would be willing to step away from the work with the kids, we can ask your parents for permission for you to ride along with our team as they help whales that are stranded near our shores. Don't get too excited—you won't be doing any of the boating, swimming, or disentangling. You'll be sitting in the boat taking notes as the crew does that real work."

Mac's hand shot into the air. Suddenly, whale watching didn't seem so boring after all. Not compared to another four days of cleaning pee and handing out whale worksheets and nautical-themed graham crackers.

Tuesday

ALIA AND SIMON WERE AT IT AGAIN, CRACKING jokes, being silly, and blaring music.

"What's your zine about?" Lina asked Avery.

"I don't really know," Avery said, pasting a picture of Angela Davis on top of a picture of an ice cream sundae. "I'm just taking pictures that make me happy and then going from there. I guess I'm trying to figure out what makes me happy." She kind of laughed. "What about you?"

"I think I want to make something for Milo. For his going away. I don't know what, though." She frowned a little, then felt the surprising urge to cry. She swallowed hard and stared at the ceiling. She would not cry, not in front of Avery, not in front of Alia and Simon. She would be happy for him, because what kind of sister wouldn't be happy for this amazing opportunity? What kind of sister would want her genius brother to sit home without the chance to get a life-changing education just so that they could be sitting home together? A monster. She pasted a smile on her face.

"Maybe something in every single language in the world." Avery half laughed again.

"Yeah, I mean, I think I want to make something that feels like it could only come from me. But I don't know what that is. And he's been so weird lately." *Yup, he's the only one being weird, not me,* she thought, *toooootally.*

"Milo? Weird? Your superspy brother? No way!" They both laughed for real this time.

"I know, I know, but last night? He shucked all that corn and spent like the whole afternoon with Kevin obsessing over the grill. Since when does he cook? And then an apple pie with ice cream for dessert? Like, what?" The cooking was weird, that was for sure, but what was harder to say was that it hurt her feelings. That she would do anything to get him to put down the grill tongs and spend some time with her, something that until five weeks ago, she'd never needed to ask him for—they were always just together, in and out of each other's rooms, each other's bookshelves, each other's sneakers, without even asking. And she didn't want to start now.

"Yeah, you're not wrong. He's being extra weird. But if it keeps being delicious, I do not care."

Lina let out a sigh and looked away. "And then there's the book."

"What book?"

"We've had this idea since we were like ten that when he had learned enough languages, we would make a graphic novel of *The Phantom Tollbooth* because we were both obsessed with it when we were little. We were going to make this crazy-cool version of it with a different language for every chapter. I was going to do all the drawings, and he was going to do the translation. I'm on chapter eight already, but he hasn't touched a page. They just sit on his desk collecting dust. It feels like he's off to Truegrove already, even though he's still here."

Lina had surprised herself by saying so much. Especially to Avery. Lately it'd been hard to squeak out two coherent sentences in front of her.

"Yeah," said Avery, reaching for the glue. "Change sucks. And people do too."

"Okay, sunshine," Lina said, teasing. "Maybe that's what your zine is about. Maybe it's an antidote to suckage."

"I like that," Avery said with a grin, her full focus on the page in front of her.

Lina looked up at the windows, the bright light and sea air flowing in. She still felt stuck. She watched the other kids hard at work, wondering how everyone else seemed to know how to "use their voices," like Simon said. She recognized most of the kids; a lot of them had been coming here just as long as she had. Michaela was working on a zine about horses because of course she was. Teo was making a zine about modernist art (his parents owned a gallery in town, and he imagined himself its junior docent). Curly Green Eyes, the girl who'd made Lina forget how to wear a backpack, was sitting across from her again, pasting a picture of a rainbow next to a picture of another rainbow. She looked up quickly and met Lina's gaze. She had tiny lightning bolt earrings.

"Hey," she said, a smile creeping up the corner of her mouth. She exuded cool. Too cool for a full smile, too cool for Lina, for sure.

"Hey, uh . . . that's neat. What's your zine about?" Since when did she say "neat"?

"It's like a literal interpretation of this whole thing. You know, putting the gay into gayby." Lina looked confused. "You know, like, being the gay kid of gay parents?"

"Oh." Lina smiled. "Yeah, I'm that."

"Well, That, it's nice to meet you. I'm Nat."

"Oh, no, I mean I'm Lina." She tried, hard, to

pronounce her own name correctly. Her tongue tripped a little, like it was the first time she'd ever said it.

"Hi," Nat said, her voice warm and low.

Nat looked at her work, and Lina went to the bathroom so that she could stop staring at her. When she came back to the table, Avery pulled her chair out for her.

"M'lady," she said with a curtsy.

Well, that was weird. "Um, thanks."

"I've been meaning to tell you, L, that new piercing is really cute on you."

Lina could feel her face going hot. "Thanks. They only let me get it because of Milo."

"Well, if suckage has to happen, at least you look hot."

Lina shoved her hands under her legs because she didn't know what else to do with them. First Nat flashing her green eyes at her, and now Avery acting like her knight in shining cuteness—it was all very confusing. She gripped the edge of the chair because the chair made sense.

At CCS, Milo had laid out an elaborate scavenger hunt starting at the center and then spreading across the lawn and down the sidewalks, eventually leading the campers back inside and into the life-size replica of the inside of a right whale. Mac didn't care about how Milo was insisting on continuing with his "Mr. Perfect" act, or that all the kids loved him. Mac didn't care because Mac wasn't there.

That morning, when they'd walked into CCS, Milo had turned to the right to his crowd of adoring child fans, and Mac had gone to the left, where Joe had ushered him to the Marine Animal Entanglement Response room. There, Sam, the team leader, greeted him with a nod and said, "Permission slip," holding out her hand. Mac reached into his pocket for the crumpled sheet. "Get in the car."

On the drive, nobody talked. Eventually, Mac got up the nerve to ask where they were going. If he was being kidnapped by a group of ecological do-gooders, this was probably the time to find out.

"We've got a rescue. You're going to get on the boat with us and take notes. Everything we tell you to write down, write it."

Mac's insides went cold. He'd never been good at paying attention to details or taking notes—obviously, he hadn't even been paying attention yesterday when Joe explained the job. What if he couldn't do it?

His worries didn't go away as much as they were temporarily overshadowed by all the commotion that happened when they got to the pier. Within what seemed like seconds, everyone was on the boat and it was heading out to sea. It wasn't a big boat like the ferry or the ones he'd been on whale watching; it was a small, fast, motorized raft that hurtled up and down with the bounce of the sea. The boat slowed as the sea settled, and soon they stopped entirely.

"There it is!" Gail, the other rescuer, shouted.

"Okay, kid, write down N 42° 5' 36.8154", W 70° 16' 1.365"," Sam said.

"What?" Mac's hands were sweaty, and he couldn't hear Sam over the rushing of wind in his ears.

"Tate, show him." Tate was a high school senior who was volunteering for the summer. *Great,* thought Mac, *now I get to look dumb in front of the only other kid.*

"Don't worry about Sam," said Tate. "She's tough, but it's just because she cares." Mac watched Sam dive off the boat and head out into the water, where a black fin shone above the surface.

"Have you been working here a long time? Is that how you know?"

"I've kind of been working here my whole life. Sam's my mom." *Oh, even better. Unimpressive in front of the mom and daughter at once, a familial two for one.*

"It's not too bad once you get the hang of it. Take the clipboard; always bring a pencil, never a pen."

"Why?"

"Why what?"

"Why not a pen?"

"Ink and water don't make good friends. You write in

pencil and the page falls into the ocean or it starts to rain, we still stand a chance."

"Got it." Tate really did seem like she'd been working on these boats her whole life. She explained everything, like that the numbers and letters Sam had shouted at them before getting into the water were GPS coordinates, and that those were important because they would need to come back and check on the whale again tomorrow. She explained that on the way back in, Sam would tell him about what she saw, and he would need to take notes.

"Don't try to write down every word. Mom doesn't talk much, but when she does, she talks quickly. We don't need to be able to make sense of what you write down, only you do. When we get back on land, we'll write it all down properly, but for now, whatever you need to do to capture what she's saying, do it. Pictures, abbreviations, whatever. We need to know as much as we can so that we can figure out what the patterns are, what sort of traps the animals are getting stuck in, if it's in the same area every time, that kind of thing."

"This seems kind of important. Why are you trusting it to some kid like me?"

"Listen, this is a pretty small crew—there are only two other rescuers besides my mom. We need all the help we can get, and you seem like decent help to me." She handed him the pencil.

Teachers had been on Mac about paying attention since before he could remember. At first, he tried. He would sit and think *Focus, focus, focus, focus* over and over again in class, and then that thought would turn to *F-o-c-u-s-f-o-c-u-s-f-o-c-u-s-f-o-c-u-s,* and soon that was all he could hear, and whatever it was he was supposed to be paying attention to had long since been erased off the board. In second grade, he'd figured out that if he tapped something—his feet, his hands, his pencil—then it was easier for him to follow along. But Ms. Garfield had a strict no-tapping policy (which seemed a lot more like a strict no-Mac policy), and he spent most of second grade tapping by himself in the hallway.

Eventually, he stopped tapping, and he also stopped trying. He realized that most people cared way more about the tapping than about the learning, and that if he could be quiet and not try, he'd probably be just fine. And he had been, until this year. Seventh grade seemed to only require things that were hard for Mac. He was quick with patterns and didn't mind reading as long as it wasn't boring, and that had been enough to carry him through six long, boring years of school. But all of a sudden this year, teachers were on his case, calling his name in class like they were trying to prove he wasn't paying attention (he wasn't), trying to talk to him about it after class was over (he packed up and slipped out as fast as he could, but they still caught him sometimes with their worried looks and their theories about his "potential"), and his solid Bs and Cs had taken a nosedive.

At the end of May, after the worst parent-teacher

conference ever, Mom took him to a learning specialist. There were three days of what the specialist called "games" but were obviously really tests to see how dumb Mac was, and then they deemed him "2e."

"Twice exceptional," Mom explained, like it was a good thing. "It means that you're really, really smart, which we already knew, and also that you've got some learning stuff that makes it hard for you to show everything you can do. Think of it this way: you're creative, and you're perceptive, and sometimes you're creating or perceiving when your teacher wants you to be multiplying or memorizing. It's not a bad thing—it's part of what makes you special, what's always made you special."

There was nothing worse than Mom calling him special. It was like she'd been waiting basically his whole life for him to reveal his secret, magical, thoughtful, creative, passionate self, but instead he was Mac—kind of quiet, not that into it, trying to blend in. The distance between how special Mom believed he was and how unspecial he knew he was made him bristle with anger when she tried to tell him about all the ways she believed he was unique.

They could call him twice exceptional, but it wasn't going to change him into the son Mom had longed for—he already knew that. That was when he started leaving whole pages of quizzes blank and stopped doing homework entirely.

At the beginning of the summer—the day after the last day of school, to be exact—Mac and his mom walked into the principal's office. It was weird to be there without other kids, the halls light, clean, and empty, the only sound the lawn mower, the smell of sweet cut grass and hot sun coming in through the window. Dr. Nick (that's how he insisted the kids refer to him, which Mac hated and therefore called him nothing at all) informed Mac and his mother that Mac had officially failed all of his classes.

"The only option we have now, short of repeating the year, is summer school." Mom and Dr. Nothing at All stared at Mac for a long time. He was looking at his shoes and didn't realize they were waiting for him to answer until Mom softly put her hand on his. He moved his hand and looked up.

"Oh. Me?"

"You're certainly the only one who can make this decision, Mac. Summer school, or do you want to do seventh grade again?" If Mac was honest, he didn't really care that much. It would be embarrassing to have to stay back, sitting with the seventh graders instead of with his friends, but it would be easier. But he knew what he was expected to say, and so he said it.

"Summer school is fine."

"Okay. Make sure you do what you need to do, and hopefully we'll see you in eighth grade in the fall."

Until Family Week, all Mac had done all summer was go to class, go to the learning specialist, and go home. Every night, Mom insisted on sitting with him at the dining room table while he did his work.

"I'm not a baby, Mom," he would complain as she watched him work. "You don't need to sit here."

"Oh, I'm just here in case you need help," she would say, unconvincingly, as she pretended to do a crossword.

It had been a long summer so far.

But out here on the water, time seemed to fly by. Sam

and Gail climbed back onto the boat, took off their gear, and started talking. Mac gripped the clipboard, his foot tapping in time with the boat, which bounced slightly as they began the ride back to shore.

"Okay. We've got a humpback whale, adolescent male. He's entangled in fishing gear around his fluke. We've attached the keggers, and he is able to breathe on his own. We'll come back tomorrow to finish." Mac finished writing it all down just as soon as Sam finished saying it, but he was pretty sure he could recite it from memory. The feeling that he'd had when he was seven came rushing back—whales *were* majestic. Whales moved along the waves and currents: despite all that human beings had done to ruin everything from land to shore, there they were, enormous, powerful, unstoppable. But this one was stopped, and Mac's heart hurt for this whale, a feeling that was both very strange and very familiar.

"Why tomorrow?"

"Instead of today?"

"Don't you want to get him free?"

"I do. But he's a whale, kid. We can't just swim up

to him, introduce ourselves, and disentangle him. The keggers, those round red buoy things you see floating by him, will keep him near the surface and wear him out. When we come by tomorrow, he should be tired and we should be able to make some progress freeing him from the gear."

"What about sharks?" In recent years, due to climate change, sharks had become more and more common, closer and closer to the shores of Cape Cod (see previous comment about humans ruining everything). It didn't bother Mac much; he figured that as long as he kept an eye out for a fin running through the waves, or a seal (sharks' favorite snack) getting close to the beach, sharks wouldn't be too interested in him. His mother, however, disagreed and didn't let him near the water without checking her Sharktivity app first for recent reports of shark sightings.

"Most of the time, sharks leave whales alone. They're too powerful, even for a shark. But I'm not going to lie to you, kid, it's a worry. Sharks do eat whale carcasses, and this whale could be close to becoming one." Mac nodded silently. He wasn't used to the way Sam talked, like he didn't need babying, like he wasn't about to screw up, like she wasn't trying to protect him.

At the dock, Sam went to check in with some of the fishermen who would be heading out near the whale, asking them to keep an eye out for seals.

"Mac," she called as he headed away from the boats, "see you at seven a.m. Don't be late."

The beach campfire was always at Herring Cove. It was a funny mix of a place, like a lot of things in Provincetown. Herring Cove sat right on the tip of Provincetown—the tip of the tip, as it were—so you looked out into the water and saw absolutely nothing but ocean and horizon. The first half of the beach was usually overrun by families with small children. The beach was covered in rocks, which kids piled into buckets and threw into the water. If you walked as far down the beach as you could, there were no children and very few bathing suits. But the campfire was at dusk, and it was only families and a few stubborn old folks who looked like they'd gotten melted into their beach chairs sitting way out along the shoreline, waiting for the tide to carry them in. Back on the shore, Carole spread out three blankets, which started as tiny folded-up bags and ended up taut against the ground with tiny spikes, easily accommodating all nine of them. They were rainbow colored (of course), and she brought them with her every year all the way from Wisconsin. Kevin and Andrew made the same jokes they always made about how a lesbian is always prepared, and Em, Julia, and Carole teased back as they always did that without the lesbians, the gay boys would have nothing but rocks to sit on.

The campfire started with a corny concert, and the little kids shook their bodies and danced in front of the fire, reveling in the attention and applause. It was hard for Mac, Milo, Lina, and Avery to remember ever being that comfortable in their skin. Kevin and Em were chatting on one blanket, while Andrew, Carole, and Julia spread out on another. They sent the kids off to make s'mores. Each of them had a different way to roast a marshmallow. Milo stood right at the periphery, examining the fire for the perfect cozy spot that would produce a round, light brown marshmallow. Lina floated hers around the top of the flames, barely letting it warm. Mac accidentally set his on fire and swore. Avery set hers on fire on purpose and cackled at the black shell around the goo.

"Interesting technique," Nat said, appearing next to Lina. The fire sparkled in the corners of her lightning bolts. Lina tried to do two things: not audibly gasp and not drop her marshmallow into the fire from excitement.

"Fire kind of freaks me out," Lina said. Nat grinned. "I know, I know, I'm a chicken."

"That's not what I was thinking. I was thinking that you're cute."

As Lina looked up, Avery squeezed between the two of them and put her arm around Lina's shoulder. "Walk with me."

Lina was as pleased as she was annoyed as she was

surprised. Why did it seem like every time Nat came around, Avery wanted to be close to her? It felt so adult, walking down the beach together at night. It made Lina brave.

"How are you doing with everything?" she asked as she looked out at the water.

"Oh, I'm fine," Avery said with a sigh. "Not as fine as Nat, though, am I right? I saw you looking at her today."

Everything with Avery was confusing. Why put her arm around her and ask her to walk on the beach together if she was going to ask her about another girl? She made Lina feel special one moment and invisible the next. If Ma had been there, she'd have nudged Lina in the ribs.

It was time, and Lina knew it.

"Okay, what is going on, Avery?" She didn't mean to sound mad, but, well, she was kind of mad.

"What are you talking about?" Avery scrunched up her face as if to prove her own innocence and incomprehension.

"The letter."

"What letter?" Avery tried to keep her voice even, but she looked up to the sky.

The blood rushed to Lina's face, and she felt suddenly very warm, even though it was night and they were standing in six inches of cold ocean. Maybe Avery really never got it?

"I sent you a letter . . . in, um, January."

Avery was quiet for a long time. "I know," she finally said.

"So why did you say 'What letter?' like you had no idea?" Lina was shouting, but she didn't mean to be.

Avery said nothing.

"Oh," Lina said, now barely above a whisper, "because you don't want to talk about it. Because you don't like me."

Avery's eyes lined with tears. They sat at the edge of the water, letting the waves come up over freezing toes. Lina worked up the courage to ask the question that had been plaguing her all day: "Then why are you grabbing my hand, or telling me I'm hot, or trying to keep Nat as far away from me as possible? You don't have to like me, fine, but then, what, no one can?"

"It's not that I don't like you." Avery folded her hands over her knees.

"What is it, then?"

Avery took a deep breath. "Lina, my whole life just fell apart. I have no idea how I feel. Like, about anything. Do I like you? Yes, of course, I love you. As more than a friend? I don't know. I don't know what I want for breakfast. I don't know where I want to live or how I'm ever going to be able to forgive my dad or if I'll ever hear Papa's real laugh again, not the stupid, strained one he uses now. I didn't know that it was possible to hate an unborn baby, but I do. I didn't know being the mixed-race kid of an interracial, interfaith gay couple would be the most normal thing about me, but man, do I miss it.

"I never talked about it, but there were times when I was really little, like three or four, when I wanted a mom. Now it's like my dad went and got me one, just what I've always wanted, a mom, a baby sister, a straight family, and I would give everything, every single thing in me, to turn back the clock and tell three-year-old me she was an idiot." Her hands turned to fists and went straight down by her sides into the sand. She remembered coming home from preschool with the family picture that she'd drawn of herself, Papa, Daddy, their fish Cat, and a faceless woman in the corner of the page. "My mommy," she'd said when Papa and Daddy had asked about it. She remembered the stricken look on their faces, knowing she'd given the wrong answer. They grabbed their special book that they'd been reading to Avery since before she could talk, all about the special way such a special kid was born—the surrogate, the doctors, the sweet picture of her first night in her crib, one tiny hand curled around one of Daddy's big fingers, the other around one of Papa's. Avery could recite it by heart, then and now, but preschool and its incessant talk of mommies had taken hold. It was a phase, as so many things are with little kids—for example, she no longer wanted a little sister, despite begging for one when she was seven, or to be an astronaut.

"I think most of us feel that way from time to time when we're little. It's hard having a family that's different."

"Yeah, well, I've gotten my wish and it's ruined my life. And Papa's life. Do you see his face? He's a mess."

"I know."

"So anyway, I don't know if I like you. I do know that I love you, and I know more than anything that I cannot take one more inch of change right now. Okay?" Avery rested her head on Lina's shoulder, and Lina let her.

"Yeah. But then, if you want to just be my friend, can you just act like my friend? No more grabbing me or flirting with me?"

"I will try to resist."

"Avery! That's what I'm talking about!" She playfully pushed Avery's head away.

"Yes, yes, okay. I'll stop."

"Is that why you're being so weird about Nat?"

"No. I just don't trust her. It's a vibe. She's just sooooo cool. I get that it's nice to have someone like you, I get that it's simpler than liking me, but you should stay away."

"You don't even know her!"

"I know what she's like."

"Like what?"

"Like me. But worse. Because I might be confused, but she's just messing with you for fun."

"Oh, because it's so impossible that someone cool might like me?"

"That's not what I meant."

"How am I supposed to trust a shoplifter, anyway?" She regretted it the second she said it. It was so dark, Lina didn't see Avery get up as much as she felt it. She watched her angry shadow storm past her dads and then into the parking lot. Lina kicked the sand off her feet and into the ocean. The wind kicked back into her own face, which seemed about right. If this had been a TV show, Lina would have thought that Avery was just jealous—if it had been a show, she might even have had an encouraging best friend who would tell her so. But Avery *was* her best friend, and of all the things she was, including a thief, she wasn't a liar and she was hardly ever wrong.

Wednesday

THE SECOND SHE OPENED HER EYES, LINA KNEW Avery was missing. She could feel it. Lina threw on clothes and ran downstairs. Andrew and Carole were sitting at the table, sipping tea and staring at their phones.

"Where's Avery?"

"Oh, she texted saying she was spending the night with a friend from home," said Andrew absently.

"Which friend?" Lina tried to keep the worry out of her voice, but she failed.

Andrew looked up, curious at her sharp questioning. "Maggie."

Maggie. The girl from their first day there, the one Avery literally hid in the bathroom to avoid. How could parents be so clueless? No reason to worry them. Since Andrew apparently hadn't realized that his own daughter was lying, missing, or both, Lina would go find her herself.

"Off to camp early? Have a good day!" Carole called after her.

Lina took off on her bike into town. At every corner, she looked down the skinny alleyways between houses, but she had a feeling Avery wasn't in the usual spots. The log outside Angel Foods was empty, nobody on the benches by Spiritus. She dumped her bike by the candy shop and walked out to the beach in the back. There were folks fishing and eating breakfast on the patio, but no Avery. Back on her bike, Lina rode past the new hipster coffee shop, the old hipster coffee shop, the record store that always blared dance music but never sold any records, the fancy West End market that only sold vegan wraps and protein shakes. She'd been out this far before, but not that often, and never alone. *Keep going,* a voice inside her said.

And so she did, taking a right off Commercial all the way to Route 6 and then a left. The whole time, one part of her brain told her that this was crazy, there was no way Avery was all the way out here. The other part of her brain told her that of course she was. Each pedal stroke brought an opposite thought. She shook her head to quiet them and pushed faster.

The tip of Cape Cod split in two: Herring Cove on one side, Race Point on the other. Herring Cove was on the bay side—little waves, big rocks. Race Point was on the ocean side, and it was hard to believe that two such different beaches could be right next to each other. At Race Point, the waves crashed onto the soft sand, ringing in your ears or knocking you on your butt. They'd spent most of last Family Week there, finally brave enough to handle the big waves. Milo, Lina, and Avery spent a whole lot of time in the surf. It was Mac who swam out and didn't come in until every finger and toe had turned full-on prune.

Lina threw her bike down in the parking lot and trekked up the dunes. It was only eight a.m.—hardly anyone on the beach but some runners and a mom with a very energetic three-year-old. Avery sat completely still at the spot where the dark sand met the light, legs tucked inside her hoodie, arms around her legs. Lina sighed with relief. She walked across the beach and sat down next to Avery without saying a word.

"Why are you bothering to look for a thief?" Avery spat out. Lina put her arm around Avery, leaning her head on Avery's shoulder. Avery was still beautiful, of course, but right now all Lina could see was the seventeen different kinds of pain she was in. She didn't need an admirer; she needed a friend. There were no sparks this time as Avery's cold body squeezed close to Lina's warm one. No electricity running up and down her arms.

"Come on. We're getting breakfast."

When Milo and Lina were little, they'd had this twin radar that woke them both up at the same time every day. Milo would wake up with his brain whirring a million miles a minute around four forty-five a.m., and Lina's eyes would pop open at the same time. Mom and Ma would take turns dealing until they were old enough to deal by themselves. When it was Mom's turn and it was Family Week, they would deal at Chach. Chach was a diner out by the Stop & Shop, away from the busyness of Commercial Street, more interested in the locals than in the tourists, and had the best breakfast in town by a landslide. In this particular moment, it had the added benefit of being the first open restaurant they would pass coming back into town from the beach, which was good because Lina was going to be just as tired as Avery pretty soon, after pedaling for miles down Route 6 with Avery on her handlebars. Not to mention the exhaustion that comes after a whirlwind of worry and fear subsides. It was like she could feel the adrenaline leaving her body by the second and weariness taking its place.

"So," Lina said, sliding into the booth and resting her elbows on the cool blue tabletop. "You slept there?"

"Yeah, I'm a real nature girl," said Avery sarcastically.

"You really freaking scared me." Lina closed her eyes hard to keep the tears from coming. It didn't work. Of course the waitress appeared at that second. Avery ordered them pancakes, orange juice, and two sides of bacon. Lina chewed on the ice cubes in her water glass.

"What do you care what happens to a common thief?" Avery asked once the waitress had left.

"Okay, first of all, there's nothing common about you," Lina said with a teary smile. Avery choked on the water she was drinking as she tried to keep herself from laughing. "And I'm sorry I said that. I do trust you. But I think you're wrong about Nat."

"I'm not. But that's fine. And you don't have to trust me. But I've met girls like Nat before—so have you.

Remember Lacey?" Lacey had come to Family Week last summer. She was heading into ninth grade but still made time for Avery and Lina, even though they were lowly rising seventh graders. She invited them out with her older friends from home, she took them with her to a completely unsanctioned nighttime bonfire on the beach—and Avery and Lina footed the bill for the cab, begged their parents for money to bring snacks, even stole some of the underappreciated beers from the fridge for Lacey and her friends. But that night, as Lacey drank their parents' beer with her friends, she left her phone on the picnic blanket next to Avery. *I have to bring the babies, but don't worry, they're good for snacks and beer,* read the first text. They left the party, quiet and embarrassed, and Lacey never spoke to them again.

"I don't think this is really about Lacey, or Nat, or even me. And for the record, looking for your body this morning and hoping you were alive was not great."

"I didn't mean to scare you. . . ." The food came, and for a moment there was no talking as they split the pancakes, covered them in syrup, swallowed their juice in one gulp, and burned their fingers on the hot bacon.

Once they came up for air, Lina asked, "You meant to scare your parents?"

"Yeah. Or test them, I guess? Anyone who knows me knows that Maggie Reiner is not exactly my sleepover buddy."

"I know. Do they know how bad it's been?" Lina had this way of asking questions—staring straight at you, pouring love right from her eyes into yours. Avery had to answer.

"Yeah, I guess. They're both kind of distracted at the moment by how bad it is for them. Which is, granted, super freaking bad. I get that. It's just, like, they've been so scared *of* me. Not scared *for* me, just scared that I would be mad at them. Of course I'm mad at them! But then they handle me like I'm this about-to-erupt thing, this thing they're scared to touch, or look at, or talk to. I don't want to be that scary, not to them." Avery took a deep breath.

"So you decided to test them?" Lina said, kind eyes unflinching.

"Yeah, and they failed. I just scared my best friend instead."

"That me?" Lina asked happily.

"Yeah, dummy, that's you," Avery said.

"I accept your apology."

"Excellent." Avery had been allergic to the actual word "sorry" since Lina had known her—so, basically since she could talk.

"Can I ask you a question?"

"You want to know why I steal lip balms? It's a fair question. Well, first of all, it's usually lipsticks. Second, I want them to notice. I want them to freak out, or get mad, or just . . . notice. And if I can't do that, then . . . It's hard to explain. It feels so good and so bad at the same time. It's like I'm finally in charge of something in my life. It's also like I have a reason to feel as bad as I do, because I'm a bad person."

"Avery, you're not a bad person. I've known you your whole life, practically. You're not bad. But the person you're scaring isn't them, it's you." Avery flicked a tear away from the corner of her eye. "Let's get you home."

They each held one of the handlebars as they made their way from Chach to the East End.

Before they walked in the house, Lina said, "You're going to have to tell them. You know that, right? I can't let you get eaten by a coyote while you're waiting for them to get it together. By Friday, or I'll do it myself." Avery nodded again. Lina gave her a long hug and put a glass of water by her bed. Of all the scenarios she'd practiced in all the health classes she'd ever been in, she still didn't feel prepared for this one. Was she doing the right thing? Should she go shake Andrew and Kevin right now and get them to see Avery nearly imploding? Should she watch her sleep to make sure she didn't go away again? In health class, the answers were so easy: get an adult, ask for help, don't do it on your own. But what if on her own was the best bet for keeping Avery safe? She lay down on the couch in the living room, resting her head against the old cushions and the hard wicker, close enough to Avery's room to hear the door creak if it opened.

Avery woke around lunchtime, saw Lina passed out on the couch, and smiled. She wandered to the empty kitchen.

"Hey," said Mac, walking through the door. "Where've you been?"

"Long story. Where have you been?"

"Oh, you know, rescuing whales, no biggie."

"I need to hear all about that," Avery said, perplexed.

Mac smiled, grabbing the bread and starting to make sandwiches for both of them without asking if she was hungry. Of course she was hungry. He wanted to tell her about the water and the waves, watching Sam and Gail take apart the jigsaw puzzle of ropes, each layer revealing a happier, calmer whale. And then that moment when the whale finally breached, blowing water everywhere, and swam on. How Mac had never been so happy, and how weird it felt to know that was true, and how, yes, he knew that he just three days ago threw a total fit about going on a whale watch, but this was different, so maybe it wasn't really about the whale watch, but this was totally different anyway, and when he watched the big blue-and-black body surface and swim, he felt all of his own muscles stretch and soar too. But he wasn't sure he could find the words.

"I think I need to hear all about why you look like what the cat dragged in," Mac said instead.

"What does that mean?" Avery asked, semi-offended and mostly laughing.

"I don't know—it's just something my mom says. Here, eat a sandwich."

"I will eat your sandwich, and then we're going to go do something fun," said Avery. "We could both use some fun."

"What's that?"

"Bloff blee," said Avery through a mouthful.

"I'll see?" repeated Mac. "Oh, great."

Avery texted Lina a heart, told her to sleep, and promised to be home for dinner.

The drag workshop was happening in the Crown & Anchor, which was funny enough to begin with. Usually a club filled with sweaty, dancing men, it had been taken over as a Family Week event space, and the queens from Drag for Kids were standing in front of the room shouting instructions and pointing this way and that like born camp counselors.

Mac hissed at Avery, "Gabber, what in the world are we doing here?"

"Chin up, Goober, or everyone will think you're some homophobe. A little drag never hurt anyone."

Everyone was starting to take seats in front of the queens, who were holding clipboards and asking for attention. Mac groaned, but he followed Avery to the back row.

"Children," said one, clapping her hands together, "welcome to the Drag Family Workshop. I'm your host, Kiki Wylde, and this is my good Judy—for those of you who are future heterosexuals of America, that means friend—Coco O'Plenty."

"Good afternoon, children." Coco put her hand to her ear. "I didn't hear you."

"Good afternoon, Coco," they all said, through giggles, in unison.

"That's better. Now let's get down to business."

Business, it turned out, would be designing a drag persona (of any gender, or none at all), getting a drag name, and beating your face. ("Don't worry, babies, it won't hurt a bit"—it turned out "beating a face" just meant putting on makeup. Mac wasn't entirely sure which was worse.)

"Drag is about being free. It's about being yourself, but yourself turned up to a thousand. Yourself without any of the things that make being you hard. Everybody close your eyes. I said, *everybody* close your eyes." Mac's face went hot. He closed his eyes. "I want you to imagine what you would do if you weren't afraid of anything. I want you to imagine a time you felt really, truly free."

Mac felt the wind and sun on his face, the rush of the

water. He imagined going out to the whale with Sam and Tate, wet-suited and unafraid.

"Whatever it is you're thinking about right now in this moment, whatever it is that's making you smile even if your grumpy little self got dragged here by your friend and didn't even want to come"—Mac opened one eye and smiled just a little—"condragulations, baby, that's your drag." Mac wasn't sure that a wet suit could count as drag, but if drag was about being your truest, most fearless self, he knew what he needed to do. But he wasn't sure, at all, that he could do it or how. He did know that he wouldn't tell anyone until he could figure it out.

Back at the house, Milo was chopping onions.

"There's an easier way to do that. Want me to show you?" Mom came around the island, and Milo passed her the knife.

"You cut along the line of the onion, just little slits. Now like this," she said, turning the onion around. "Et voilà!" Mom picked up the perfectly diced pieces to show him.

"Nice French," Milo said.

"Listen, smartie, my fifth-grade French still serves me well, merci very much." Milo laughed. "What's on le menu tonight?"

"I don't know—I was thinking about maybe pork chops or chana masala or, like, carnitas?"

"Wow, really traveling the culinary globe there."

"Yeah." Milo hung his head. "I don't know."

"You've been cooking a lot this week."

"Yeah, you know, I'm about to be on my own. I've gotta be able to cook."

Mom squeezed his shoulder. He could feel her keeping herself from saying anything.

"I'm fine, Mom."

"I know you are. But also, this isn't your last week with us. You don't have to put so much pressure on yourself to make it perfect, to be perfect. You're just right—"

"Just the way I am. I know, Mom."

When Milo started speaking full sentences at nine months old, his parents got some books on gifted children. Milo had read them himself from time to time (starting when he was three, Lina liked to joke). They knew that perfectionism could be the downfall of gifted children, that they were so used to doing everything right the first time that they had a low frustration tolerance, that anything that didn't come naturally felt like failure. Ma handled that by never, ever letting Milo win, not at Candy Land, not at basketball, not at *Sonic the Hedgehog*. Mom handled it by telling Milo that he was just right just the way he was, like, all the time.

"You don't have to talk to me about it if you don't want to, honey. But you and I both know that all this cooking, all this planning of scavenger hunts for children you don't know, it's all lovely, but it's all keeping you from the person you actually need to talk to."

He knew she meant Lina. He knew that he was hurting her, being distant and weird. And the book. He had to get started on the book. There were only a few weeks left. But that's exactly why he couldn't get started. It felt like once he started with "Érase una vez un muchacho llamado que no sabía qué hacer consigo mismo: no sólo a veces, sino siempre," it would all be over. In his brain, his big smart brain, there was this tiny fantasy that if he never finished the book, he would never go to Truegrove. He tried to keep that thought quiet and far away—and tried keeping away anything that made him long to stay home, like Lina. Instead, he replayed the conversations, the many conversations, that he'd had with parents, teachers, and anyone else who found out about the amazing classes, free ride, opportunity of a lifetime, too-good-to-turn-down offer that he had at the country's best boarding school.

"I'm going to make tacos. I need the comal." And he busied himself with looking in cabinets for a flat pan that they both knew the house didn't have.

♡

"Yes, henny!" Kevin and Andrew shouted at Mac and Avery as they sat down at the table for tacos with their glitter eye shadow and fake nails. Avery glowered at them, but Mac smiled.

"Your daughter is a terror. She told me we were going for a walk, and look at me now."

"Been there," said Lina quietly, and Avery shot her a smile.

"You look great," said Kevin. "Talent show, here you come."

"I guess you'll have to wait and see," said Mac coyly. Milo nearly choked on his own taco. Coy, smiling Mac instead of grouchy, sullen Mac was such a surprise, Carole entirely forgot about her Sharktivity app and her plan to lecture Mac at dinner about water safety while he was out with the disentangling team. Instead, Lina was standing next to her now, pointing to something on her phone with a grin.

"Attention, please," said Carole. "We would like to inform you of the imperative need to finish your tacos and get in the car. It's going to rain tomorrow, which means tonight is our last night to . . ."

"Drive-in!" shouted Lina, waving jazz hands at the table.

"What's playing?" asked Em.

"Who cares?"

"Um, the person who's paying for your ticket?"

"Let me put this in language you'll understand, Ma: the content of the movie is immaterial and outside of your scope of interest, counselor."

"That's your child," said Julia with a laugh. "Get the bug spray—let's go."

Every summer, one night over dinner, someone would declare it time to go to the Wellfleet Drive-In and then this exact chaos ensued: the hunt for bug spray, the change into layers so as to avoid getting eaten to death by mosquitoes, the search for lawn chairs and then blankets, the shuffling around of who would sit in which car and how many cars to take and who would follow whom so as not to get separated in line. It was messy and joyful, and one of Lina's favorite parts of the trip. Mac could be grumpy, and Milo could be weird, and Avery could be actively courting crime and tempting kidnappers, but this was Family Week, and so they would go to the drive-in.

"I think I'll sit this one—" said Kevin as everyone was rushing around gathering blankets and chairs and sweatshirts.

"No," said Lina, "you won't sit it out. We're all going. All of us." She lowered her voice and looked into his eyes, feeling braver and angrier than she expected. "Listen, you want to pretend that everything's fine? You go ahead. But we both know that everything is very far from fine, especially your daughter, so take her to the movies, okay? This is Family Week, right? Now act like it." She took a breath, raising her voice from a whisper. "Ma? Where's my hoodie?" And she walked out of the kitchen.

The Wellfleet Drive-In had everything a summer could require—movies, mosquitoes, snacks, mini golf, if you came early enough, which they never did. Instead, they always came in a rush from Provincetown down

Route 6—with Carole and Mac piled into the backseat of Kevin and Andrew's car, keeping close to Em and Julia's just ahead. They pulled into spots next to each other, Carole taking folding chairs (and yes, those blankets) out of the trunk, attempting to douse each child in bug spray as they ran off to the concession stand for everything from popcorn to nachos to hamburgers to Skittles. They came back teetering under a mountain of snacks and slushies.

"Mac seemed happy today," Andrew said to Carole as she arranged and rearranged.

"I think so," she said. "Maybe drag was the missing link the whole time?" They laughed. After a moment, she said, "You know, on the ferry here he kept saying that this would be his last Family Week. But I can see he's having a good time. I don't know what gets into him sometimes."

"Avery was saying the same."

"She was? That's interesting. I wonder what's—" Before Carole could have the chance to ask Andrew if there was something going on for Avery, or offer any of the sworn-to-secrecy information about Mac's year in school, Milo appeared by her side.

"Can I help you with that folding chair, Carole?" he offered. "Here, we got too much popcorn." He handed her a bucket the size of her head. The adults took their seats in the folding chairs. When they were little, Em and Julia would lay down blankets in the back of their Subaru, and the kids would all crawl inside to watch the movie in their pajamas, occasionally spilling slushies and M&Ms onto the blankets beneath them as they fell asleep with straws in their mouths or chocolate melting in their hands.

"Get in!" called Lina from where she was folding herself into thirds to be able to fit in the hatchback like when she was seven. Milo, Mac, and Avery just stood where they were, Milo talking to the grown-ups, Avery and Mac talking to each other. She unfolded herself with surprising ease and jumped from the edge of the car to right behind Mac's and Avery's shoulders. "Perhaps you didn't hear me. I said, GET IN THE CAR."

"Lina—" Mac started to make an excuse.

"No, she's right, Goober. Get in the car. Last one in has to give me all their snacks!" And Avery flung herself into the trunk with a thud. "What about you, Milo? Are you coming or are you too much of an adult to hang out with us now?"

"Huh?" said Milo, distracted.

"GET IN THE CAR, MILO!" yelled Avery from the trunk.

"We're sitting in the car, Milo. You know, like we have at the drive-in for the last nine summers." Lina turned back to the car, folded her knees up to her shoulders, and piled into the back between Avery and Mac.

"Oh, uh, sure, I'll come . . . ," said Milo, and he clumsily stepped on Mac's snacks and Avery's feet and thumped down next to a precariously balanced slushie. He looked at Lina and felt words bubble through him a million miles a second. He wanted to tell her that he didn't think he was a grown-up, not too grown up for sitting in the trunk, not too grown up for being her twin, not too grown up for any of it. In fact, since he had decided to go to Truegrove, he had felt more tiny and frightened than he had ever felt in his life, including the three years that he woke her up every night screaming about his recurring snake nightmare. She would pop down from her top bunk, squeeze in next to him, and build a fortress of stuffies around both of them to keep all the snakes out of their house and out of his dreams. She was so brave—she always had been. He couldn't tell her how scared he felt all the time now, not when he was supposed to be grateful for this once-in-a-lifetime opportunity everyone was so happy for him to have. Everyone but him. He wanted to say all that, but the movie was starting, so instead, he just passed her some of his popcorn as a peace offering, but she didn't see it—it was too dark in the car.

When they got back to the house, it was past ten, but everyone had caught a second wind from the car chase at the end of the movie. Carole started making tea, Em cracked open beers for the rest of the adults, and they settled around the table for a long night of Scrabble. Avery approached as they were handing out tiles.

"Can we go to Spiritus?" she asked the table.

"Oh, honey, it's pretty late," said Julia.

"I know. I do. But . . . it's vacation. And we're thirteen now. We won't be gone for more than an hour. Who knows how many more Family Weeks we—"

Kevin raised an eyebrow at Andrew, who was taking an awfully long time rearranging his letters.

Lina appeared by Avery's side. "As we, the children, grow older, it's developmentally appropriate for us to experience independence, and limits. We have to carve out our own traditions and identities, while maintaining close ties to home. For us to persist in intergenerational harmony, you must do what you must do—play Scrabble—and we must do what we must do, which is go people watch and eat ice cream." Lina got nervous as her speech came to an end. "Please?"

"Nice try, Dr. Freud," said Em.

"Give us a minute, honey," said Julia. The adults conferred while the kids pretended to give them space to talk.

"Okay," said Carole. "We've decided."

"Go," said Andrew.

"But if you're not back here by eleven sharp," Carole continued, "we're all dressing up in our most embarrassing outfits and walking down Commercial screaming your names. When we find you, we will walk hand in hand all the way back home singing. We will record it and send it to all of your friends, and you will be viral sensations throughout the World Wide Web. Are we clear?" A chorus of four yeses, muffled laughter at the parents' ancient language, and they were out the door, into the hot summer night.

♡

Sitting on dark bricks still warm from the sun, Milo looked up at the stars as his ice cream melted onto his hands.

"Uh, hey, genius boy, you've got Rocky Road all over your hands." Mac passed him a napkin.

"Oh, thanks," said Milo.

Mac and Avery were discussing the drag workshop, and she was clearly beginning to hatch a plan to get him to perform with her in Friday night's talent show.

"Come on—I'll write the song, you can perform it. They'll never see it coming."

"I'm performing in drag? In front of humans? No, thank you, Avery." They both laughed. Mac looked up at the stars, and after a moment, he asked, "Are you doing okay with it?"

"With what, the destruction of my family and the creation of this new hellscape I have to live in and pretend is a good thing because babies are cute?" Mac nodded. "I mean, not really. I don't know. If one were a child psychologist, one might say I've been doing a bit of acting out."

"One might," laughed Mac.

"You've noticed?"

"You talk to your dads like they're your servants, you're even angrier than I am, and I'm ninety-nine percent sure you didn't come home last night. You don't have to tell me about it, but yeah, I've noticed, Gabber."

Avery hung her head. "I slept at the beach. Lina found me in the morning. She thought I was dead. I told my dads I was sleeping at that girl Maggie's house, which they believed. It's like they don't even know who I am anymore." A rock appeared in her throat and traveled its way up to her eyes, making them fill with tears.

Mac reached over and threw his arms around her, holding her tight. "I promise you, we'll get them to know," he said into her ear.

Two seats down, Milo's ice cream dripped onto Lina's drawing of the public bathrooms across the street, which looked oddly beautiful in the moonlight.

Lina looked up from her sketchpad and nudged him in the ribs. "What's going on with you?"

"Huh?"

"You are so out to lunch."

"Out to ice cream, actually."

"Yes, thank you, Mr. Literal Translation."

"Ouch," said Milo, smiling.

"Seriously, what's going on? I feel like you've barely spoken since we got here. We have so little time left, and I can't get you to spend any of it with me. It's like you're too good for me now that you've got this new life waiting for you."

"That's not it." Milo shook his head. He wanted to cry. He wanted to tell her everything that was overflowing inside him. But all he could do was shake his head unconvincingly.

"Yeah, okay."

"It's just been a busy few days."

"Yeah, I can't help noticing how busy you've been. Too busy to even talk to me." Lina looked straight at Milo, expecting an answer. He looked up suddenly, and Lina turned to see what had him distracted.

"Too busy to talk to you? Never," said Nat, sitting down right next to Lina. "Hi. I'm Nat."

"Nice to meet you," said Milo icily. He got a weird vibe from Nat. He didn't like the way Lina obviously melted in her presence, that was for sure, but he had to admit that he was relieved to have her attention off him.

"So you're an artist, right?" Nat asked Lina.

"I mean, I wouldn't go that far, but I like to draw." Lina liked to draw, but she didn't like to talk about drawing. At all.

"Show me your stuff." Nat put her face near Lina's. "See, I knew you were an artist. Draw me next."

Lina hesitated, blushed against her will, and then picked up her pencil and turned to a new page in her notebook. It was a relief to not have to steal quick glimpses at Nat but instead be given full permission to stare, to memorize the shapes of her freckles, to take in every turn and crease and arch of her face.

"Told you you were an artist," Nat said. "Let me see the rest." And she looked through her pages, asking about the different designs and drawings, friends and strangers Lina had tried to capture in her pages.

"Oh my god, is that Alia? She is such a goddess."

"Yeah," said Lina. "I knew I wouldn't be able to get

her whole divine presence thing onto the page, but I had to try."

"Not bad," said Nat, and then she kissed Lina on the cheek. "See you tomorrow, Rembrandt."

Nat hopped down the stairs, leaving just as quickly as she had appeared. Lina's left cheek turned bright red first, and the rest of her face followed soon after. Avery's eyes followed Nat's back like daggers as she dodged and weaved her way down Commercial Street.

Thursday

WHEN THEY WERE LITTLE, RAINY DAYS ON THE Cape were for watching movies, convincing their parents to take them to the candy store, and a desperate excursion to the game shop on Commercial Street just to break up the boredom. When the rain woke Mac up Thursday morning, popcorn for breakfast and afternoon jigsaw puzzles were not on his mind. He threw on his uniform and headed out.

Sam and Tate met him at the door of CCS. "We've got to go. Get in the truck." Sam talked on the way to the docks. "It was a bad night. We got a call about three finbacks, a mom and her calves. This isn't going to be easy."

When they got out onto the water, Mac knew what Sam meant. He couldn't tell if the water was coming from the sky or from the splashing waves. "The call came from pretty close to shore. It's not a good sign, if I'm honest, kid," said Sam as she slowed the motor. "I'm going to stop us here. Gail's already out here with the Roughwater, paddling around looking. We don't want to run the motor and miss something—visibility is crap."

They sat in silence for a few minutes, pretending to try to see through binoculars that were only showing rain on top of water.

"What's a Roughwater?" Mac whispered to Tate.

"It's an inflatable like this one, but it's slightly more of a boat than this, which is pretty much just a raft with a motor. She's using it so that she doesn't tip over." All they could see was gray on gray on gray and then suddenly a huge splash of white, and a splash of water right on top of Sam and Mac, as Gail's Roughwater pulled up next to them.

"Okay, guys. Nothing's happening today. We can try again tomorrow when the sea's a little calmer. Also, Sam, you're getting green around the gills. Time to go in," Gail explained.

Mac hadn't noticed that Sam had been clutching the rubber side of the inflatable with both hands. They followed Gail to the dock. Sam looked woozy as she pulled herself out of the raft and tied it and the Roughwater to the pier.

"Gail—" Mac started.

"What? I can't hear you!" Gail shouted through the wind.

"I'm going to stay and watch from the pier. I know we can't see anything, but that way I can radio you two if anything changes. I just . . . I don't want to miss the window to be able to save these guys if the weather lightens up or if sharks start to circle."

Gail looked at him, squinting. Mac wasn't sure if it

was because she hadn't heard him or because she thought he was losing his mind.

"Okay, kid. That's a good idea. Here." She handed him an extra poncho and her binoculars. Her voice was firm, as it always was, but there was something new in it too, something like pride.

Mac wasn't sure what had made him say it, but there was something about the rough seas and the quick clouds that he wasn't ready to leave yet. And if it meant that he might catch sight of the whale and her babies, it would be worth hours of sitting in wet shorts. Honestly, it would be worth it anyway. The sea rocked back and forth as his feet dangled above it. It felt strange to say, but sitting on a wet dock looking out at the ocean in the middle of a storm was the thing that other people got out of meditation or yoga or whatever. Peace.

Thunder clapped in the distance.

At the library, the rain hit against the window, giving more beats to the music they were listening to. Thunder grew closer, and it seemed to Lina like a very good and lucky thing to be inside and warm, sitting in her usual seat across from Nat. Tomorrow was the last day of the zine workshop. Lina needed to get it together before she never saw Nat again.

Avery was watching all of it. Watching Nat watching Alia, watching Lina watch Nat. Maybe Lina was right: maybe she was just jealous of Nat's seemingly carefree flirting. Or jealous that Lina's moms would be together forever like good lesbians and Lina wouldn't have to walk through the world knowing that love is temporary.

She paged through a magazine, hoping to find something for her *Antidote to Suckage*. She found a picture of a Band-Aid. That seemed right. Stop the bleeding, but the scar's still there. The next page had an ad for who knew what—soap? Tiles? Parenting? That wasn't what mattered. What mattered was the picture that felt like a cold knife slicing right through her middle. She got up and ran to the bathroom.

Lina snapped out of her Nat-induced haze when she felt Avery's chair push back against the wall. The magazine Avery had been working from had fallen (been thrown?) to the floor. One look at the picture and Lina was on her feet. In it, a little Black girl—probably two or three—was covered in bubbles in an enormous bathtub. Her dad sat on the side of the tub, handing her a rubber ducky. They stared at each other, not at the camera, with enormous smiles and squinting eyes that screamed of their delight in each other, in bathtubs, in bubbles. Lina ran to find her friend.

"Avery," she said quietly, putting her hand on the stall door.

"Yeah." At least Lina thought that's what Avery said. It sounded more like a hollow swallow, a gasp for air.

"Let me in."

Avery opened the stall door, and for a moment she looked just like she had when she was a little kid and Mac had taken her doll, Sally, as a joke but then lost it by accident. First she had been angry and scheming her revenge, but then, after she'd loosened the joints on the oldest chair in the house and he'd fallen through it at dinner but her doll was still gone, she cried all night until she fell asleep curled up into a tiny, warm, shaking ball. Avery felt that way right now, like the most important thing to her in the world was gone and somehow she was just supposed to keep walking around like it was possible to find your way in a world that was upside down. Like you were supposed to be able to eat meals and laugh with friends and go to school and not steal things. Like it was all so simple. She sat on the bathroom floor with her arms around her knees, turning herself into the tiniest possible ball she could, though it was harder now than it used to be, with long legs and boobs.

Lina said nothing. She just got down on the floor and wrapped herself around Avery. A big ball over a smaller ball, holding her as tight as she could until the shaking stilled, the sobs turned to hiccups, and the hiccups made them both laugh.

"Take me to the drag workshop this afternoon," Lina said plainly.

"I'm sorry, I'm spilling out my heart and soul and

snot through my face, and you're like, 'Let's talk about drag queens'? Wow, Lina."

"You fool," Lina said, pulling Avery to her feet. "It's for you, not for me. I have an idea."

As they walked back to the table to gather their things, they heard giggles bouncing their way across the library. Lina knew the owner of those giggles immediately and felt her feet move faster to see whatever it was that was making Nat smile. Turning the corner, she froze. Nat held Lina's sketchpad open in her hand, pointing at her drawing of Alia.

"Oh my god, Alia, she has such a crush on you—it's, like, totally adorable." Lina couldn't believe the words coming out of Nat's mouth. Alia didn't look up from helping Michaela at the other end of the table.

"She's got one on you too, then," the girl next to Nat said. "She drew one of you on the next page."

"I know, so sweet, right?" But she said it in a way that didn't seem like she thought it was sweet at all. Like she thought that it was sweet the way a mom gets a card with scribbles all over it for Mother's Day thinks it's sweet. Sweet like the voice you use for a puppy, not for a girl you like. Lina turned to run down the stairs, her heart beating in her ears and her face burning.

"Nat, what are you doing with Lina's notebook?" she could hear Alia say, coming closer, anger and concern in her voice. Lina didn't want to hear the answer. But here it came, thunderous and mighty, right out of Avery's mouth.

"I can tell you what she's doing. She's trying to humiliate the kindest, most caring person in the world so that you'll think she's cool. It's, like, totally adorable. Don't you think? And you, Nat, you selfish, manipulative brat. You don't deserve Lina's art, you don't deserve her friendship, you don't deserve to know her, which you obviously don't, or you would know that being loved by Lina is the best thing that could ever happen to you. And you'll never know it, because if you ever so much as look in her direction again, it will be my mission to make your life a living hell. Alia, Simon, I'm sorry you both had to see this. But then again, you sure did teach me how to use my voice. Have a good day, everyone." She grabbed their bags and ran downstairs. Lina stood on the landing, her mouth open somewhere in between a sob and a smile. She held out her hand. Avery held on to it tight and didn't let go. Once outside, in the rain and the wind, they ran and ran all the way to the Crown & Anchor hand in hand.

Milo couldn't shake his weird mood. He told Joe he was sick, left the fighting six-year-olds with some substitute counselors in training, wished them luck, and walked out into the rain. It felt dramatic; it felt like a movie, letting his hair go heavy and damp across his forehead, his jeans turning dark, his sneakers squishing with every step. His feet were set in a forward stride with no particular destination. Maybe he'd walk all the way to the thunder he heard rumbling somewhere far from here. Maybe in that new land, he'd understand why something as awful as squishy sneakers felt perfect in this moment. He replayed the conversation with Lina last night, how much she wanted him to talk, and how much he wanted to tell her, but he couldn't and then they didn't talk for the rest of the night. How he stayed up in their quiet, dark room, willing his mouth to open and push all his truths out, until long after Lina's breath had slowed to a snore. At the same time, he started to replay the conversation with Mom in the kitchen, how he was missing this precious time with all his cooking and working and being helpful. He thought about the wordless pages of *The Phantom Tollbooth* that sat untouched in his backpack at the house. He went into the puzzle shop; he had no money, he was soaking wet, and he probably terrified at least three small children as he walked down the aisles. In the back, there was a two-thousand-piece jigsaw puzzle—clearly a Provincetown special—a picture of two moms and two kids doing a puzzle around a cozy kitchen table. Normally, it would have made him laugh, appreciating the clever puzzle within a puzzle, but the fist he felt trying to explode through his throat was a lot closer to a sob. He left quickly, leaving big, wet footprints on the purple carpet.

The rain was raining, the thunder was thundering, and it felt good. In his own way, Milo was raining and thundering too. He walked down the pier to see nothing but sky, rain, water falling into water. He sat down on the edge; the wet wood didn't even feel wet against his jeans. He tapped the bottoms of his shoes against the dock. The thunder cracked and Milo tried to breathe it all the way inside his ribs (yes, of course, he knew that wasn't how thunder, air, or ribs worked, but sometimes science needed to take a seat and let a kid try to swallow the sky). As he looked down to the water, for perhaps the first time in his life he didn't think first. He didn't think at all. He pushed with his wet hands off the wet wood and straight into the cold waves.

As Mac looked through Gail's binoculars at the spot

where the whale and her calves were still unmoving, he noticed a figure attempting to swim out. His heart started to beat fast—he didn't want that swimmer anywhere near his whales. He was waving his arms to draw the swimmer's attention when he recognized the familiar colors of the CCS uniform and the familiar person wearing it.

"Milo!" he screamed, but he knew Milo couldn't hear him over the water and his own gasping breaths. Milo had never been in water this cold or this choppy. He was a good swimmer, but he felt like a piece of driftwood being knocked backward and forward, up and down with every single wave.

Mac took a look at the Roughwater floating below him and he looked back at Milo, getting carried out too fast, too close to the whales, and also too close to drowning. He jumped into the boat below.

When Mac got near Milo, he cut the engine. He reached out his hands to Milo's flailing arms and pulled him aboard. Milo coughed, spitting seawater over the side. He shivered, tiny and covered in goose bumps. He'd plunged in with all his clothes on, and now they looked too big for him, and heavier than his bones could bear. Mac handed him the emergency blanket that Gail kept folded up at the bottom of the first aid kit.

"Thanks," Milo said, wrapping himself in the silvery fabric.

"You look like a hot dog."

"How did you get out here?" Milo asked quietly.

"Oh my god. You first, Milo. I'm here because I'm saving your butt. You're here because what? You saw that I was doing okay with this whale thing and figured that if dumb old Mac could do it, Milo the Genius could do it better?"

"I . . . I don't think you're dumb. And that's not why I got in."

"What is it, then?"

Milo didn't know where to begin. He shivered in his blanket. "I'm sorry," he said. The rain had reached that weird point in the storm where it started and then stopped and then started again.

"I'm supposed to be helping these whales, not

scooping you out of the ocean. You make such a big show of rescuing everyone all the time, Mr. Perfect, but I'm here because I was actually helping, and you're here because why?"

Milo looked down, feeling perfectly ridiculous in his soaking-wet clothes and hot dog wrapper. "I don't know."

"Never heard you say those words before."

"Very funny."

"It's true. Perfect Milo with his perfect answers, perfect recipes, perfect life. Literally everything you do is greeted with a chorus of ooohs and aaahs. It's like being around fireworks or the eighth freaking wonder of the natural world." The rain stopped.

Milo took a breath. "Do you hear yourself? Do you really think that being an Asian trans gayby genius is the freaking American dream? Did you really just say that my life is *fireworks*? That is the whitest white-boy crap I've ever heard. You've been mad at me since I was six years old. Why?" Milo's voice was louder than it usually got. Thunder boomed.

"Because you're freaking perfect. You're the kid my

mom wanted to have and instead she got me." Mac was shouting over the thunder, but also just shouting because it felt good because it was true and because he was sick of feeling bad for just being him.

"Have you ever thought, like, ever, about how that might feel?" Milo meant it. He wasn't angry, or not just angry, but also curious. Everyone assumed that having his brain was the best way to be, but had anyone actually thought about what it was like?

"Being a genius who can do no wrong? I've considered it, but apparently I've made different life choices." The rain started again.

"No, I mean what it's like to have people think that your brain is some freak show, some weird circus that comes to town to replace Google. What it's like to have people get mad at you for something you have absolutely no control over." Milo tossed a brave glance at Mac.

Did Mac know what it was like to have people get mad at him for something he had no control over? The words lifted all the anger right off his skin. "Only my whole life," he said, his shoulders relaxing.

"That's what I'm saying," Milo finished. Mac pulled his mouth up into the right corner. "You're so mad at me, but the truth is, we're not that different."

"Being held back in middle school isn't exactly the same as being a supergenius, last time I checked."

"Were you?" Milo asked, trying to keep the concern out of his voice.

"No. But they wanted to. I wouldn't have blamed them, I guess. I haven't really done any homework since, um, March."

"Yikes."

"Yeah. My mom said I should call you for help on my Spanish." They both laughed, just a little. The rain came down harder, the thunder cracks moving closer. Water splashed over the sides.

"Your brain doesn't fit in a box. Neither does mine. So maybe just talk to me instead of being a jerk to me all the time?"

"What?" More rain seemed impossible, yet here it was, carried in on gusts of even more wind. Mac was getting nervous but didn't want to let it show.

"I said we're the same."

"Not really. I spend all my time trying to hide the fact that my brain is different, and you spend all your time trying to show yours off with freaking crepes nobody asked for! Doesn't seem the same."

Milo clutched the side of the raft, bringing his body with him. Mac held on to his shoulder to keep him from going too far over and starting this whole keeping-Milo-from-drowning experiment from scratch.

"Wow, dude," Mac said when Milo came back up, pale and clammy. "I thought you liked crepes."

"I do! I'm just seasick. . . . Oh, you know that. You were joking."

"Correct."

"Sorry. I'm not . . ."

"Funny? I know."

"I don't even like cooking."

Mac just stared at him. "But . . . then . . . why?"

"Same reason I got in the water in the middle of a storm. Because I didn't know what else to do. I keep thinking that if I do everything right, I won't have to go to Truegrove. I know that's dumb. We're not little kids anymore. But I can't help thinking that if I can make myself indispensable, then they won't, you know . . ."

"Dispense with you?"

"I mean . . . yeah. That's what it feels like."

"You know, barf boy, maybe talk to your family instead of being incredibly annoying all the time?"

Milo cracked a smile. "Maybe. Jerk." He lurched back over the side, and Mac held on to him with both hands. As soon as Milo came up, he went back over.

"Dude, how much did you eat?"

"I didn't eat today," Milo said, heading over yet again. Mac wanted to make fun of him for getting puke all over the side of Gail's boat. When Milo came up this time, he was shivering. He went back over, head spinning as he sat up.

"Here," Mac said, passing him an oar.

"Manual labor, seriously? Way to kick a guy when he's down."

"Milo, listen to me: if you're in charge of moving

the boat, you won't puke as much. First right, then left, otherwise we'll spin in a circle and you'll hurl." Milo looked woozy, like another trip over the side might end up with him headfirst into the ocean or passed out in the raft. "Right, then left—just listen to my voice. You can do this. Right, then left." The boat moved centimeters, not even inches, but Milo sat up a little straighter. "Right, then left."

"How do you know what to do? Why aren't you freaking out?"

"Freaking out doesn't help mal de mer, buddy, but controlling the boat does. Right, then left."

"Mal de mer?"

"Seasickness. I thought you knew French?"

"If you make me laugh, I might puke." Milo smiled.

"Right, then left." He led them away from the whales. "So what did you mean when you said it was the same thing that got you to jump into the ocean in the middle of a storm?"

"I left CCS today. I just couldn't do it. Being perfect,

like you call it, wasn't helping. So I went for a walk in the rain, and I was sitting on the pier and . . . I wasn't anymore."

"You know, I think it might be easier to talk to us than to try to drown or get eaten by a shark," Mac said.

"I wasn't trying to do that. I was just trying to not think."

"I know what that's like," said Mac, "but, for real, there are easier ways. And not to sound like my mom, but heavy rainfall can bring sharks closer to the shore." Milo laughed, but Mac suddenly didn't. A shift in the water let Mac know there was another ship, a much bigger ship, approaching. Then a loud squeal, like the crack of a loudspeaker too close to a microphone.

"This is the United States Coast Guard," a voice said. The voice sounded official, like it wore a gleaming badge and crisp uniform. "You must return to the dock immediately. I repeat, you must return to the dock immediately."

Mac's heart sank straight to the bottom of the ocean floor. He had basically stolen Gail's boat, and now the freaking Coast Guard was here to rescue reckless Mac, who had messed up again. Mac turned the Roughwater around. As they approached the dock, Mac's worries only got worse. What had at first seemed like a bunch of disheartened tourists, or even some disgruntled workers on their break, revealed a more particular shape—that of Sam, Gail, Tate, Avery, Lina, and every single one of their parents.

Friday

THE CONVERSATION WHEN THEY GOT HOME from the docks had been brief, one of those where everyone had been too mad to talk in the moment and the boys were sent upstairs as soon as they got home.

Mac was dreading what was waiting for him at CCS. As he got dressed and snuck out the kitchen, all he could imagine was Sam, red-faced, demanding he return his uniform and never darken her doorway again. Or worse, stone-faced Gail, refusing to speak to him, letting him know exactly how much of her trust he had irreparably broken. Maybe the Coast Guard would be waiting to tell him that he could never go out on the water again. Each version felt worse than the one before. As he got closer to CCS, his mind overflowed with loud thoughts, thundering over and over: *You'll never go out on the water again.* It wasn't that he couldn't imagine his life without the sun in his face and salt on his skin, it was that he knew that life all too well. And he didn't want to go back.

He knocked on Sam's open door.

"Why are you knocking? The door's open. Don't be weird." Mac gulped. Things were just as bad as he thought.

"Sam, I just wanted to say—"

"What? You're sorry?" She wasn't looking up. Mac stared at his still-soggy shoes.

"Yeah. I really am."

Sam let out a laugh that took Mac by surprise. "I know you are, kid, but you can keep your sorry. Sit."

Mac sat on the metal folding chair across from Sam, and she shoved a brochure into his hands. "Read this."

Mac found Milo with the other counselors, passing out snacks.

"Nerd boy, I need you," Mac whispered from the hallway.

"I guess that's a step up from barf boy."

"I wouldn't go that far. Regardless, you need to call out sick."

"I can't just abandon my responsibili—"

"You did yesterday and every single child survived. *You* almost didn't, and here you are, thanks to me, so come on. You, me, and our very special brains. Now."

Mac dragged Milo into an empty classroom. He sent a text to the Family Week Crew: *Dinner at 5pm before the talent show. Don't be late.*

⭐

A five-minute walk and a universe away, Avery was nervous.

"Are you sure about this?" she asked as Lina rifled through button-downs and suspenders, trying to find the right combination.

"Of course I'm sure."

"Does it matter that I'm not?"

"Not even a little."

Coco and Kiki stopped by everyone's stations to check on them. Kiki was "beat for the gods," as she told the group when they arrived, in awe of her sparking gold eyelashes, her nose that seemed to come to a cartoonish point ("It's called contouring, children"), and cheekbones that could cut through all the emotions fluttering through the room. Coco was in what she called "boy drag," a muscle shirt, cut-off jeans, and heels. She had eyeliner on and some lip gloss, but not a full face and no chest plate.

"Nerves?" Kiki asked as Avery stared in the mirror.

"You could say that," Avery replied.

"She's going to be great," Lina said, "but this outfit is just not working. I don't think drag king is her look."

"Remember, kittens," Coco said, "drag isn't about gender. Drag is about getting free. What do you need to get free from, Avery?" Avery hung her head, and Coco put her warm hand on her shoulder.

"I've got this," said Lina. "Where are the feathers?"

"Baby, we're drag queens. You want feathers? We've got feathers."

"What is happening to me?" Avery cried, but she sounded like herself for the first time in months.

When Lina and Avery got home, Avery went upstairs to practice, and Lina wandered into the very quiet, very hot kitchen.

"Hey, Lina," said Mac. "Dinner's in twenty."

"Okay," said Lina. "Where's Milo?"

"He's outside. I kicked him out because he was bugging me and I just need a few minutes of peace to get everything plated." Lina looked confused but didn't say anything. She just walked through the screen door to find her brother, who had been so hard to find lately.

"Hey," she said quietly.

"Hey," said Milo.

"What are you doing?"

"Nothing, just sitting."

This was too awkward to bear, so Lina turned around to head back inside. "I'll let you do that, then."

"No," Milo said softly first, then loudly, "no. Lina, please stay." He looked up and into her eyes, and she sat in the big wooden chair next to his, the ones they used to pretend were sailboats when they were little, and they were mermaids washed ashore.

"Okay. Fine. I'm sitting."

"I'm sorry."

"What are you sorry for, Milo? Scaring me half to death, nearly getting arrested by the Coast Guard, or being such a stranger to me that I don't even know why you were in that boat to begin with?"

"Well, all of it, but mostly that last one."

"So why? Why have you been shutting me out even before you leave?" Tears streamed down her face, though she didn't know if she was sad or mad or both. Milo got quiet. He wanted to stay quiet, but he knew that if he did, he would push Lina even further out of reach. Maybe too far.

"Because I don't want to go, Lina! I'm sorry—I know that you're so excited for me, and I know that this is what I'm supposed to want, and I know that this is what I'm supposed to do, and I know I'm not supposed to waste my gifts, and I should be more grateful, but I'm not grateful, I'm scared and I'm angry. I don't want to let you guys down. I know you're excited for me, and this is a big chance, and I know you're excited to say your brother goes to Truegrove, and I don't want to not live up to my potential or whatever, but I don't want to go." Milo was crying now. Lina hadn't seen him cry in months.

She sat in silence for a moment, stunned. "Wow, Milo," she said, barely suppressing the laugh that was pushing through her smile.

"I know," he said, shaking his head, face red with shame.

"For such a smart kid, you really are a dummy." Milo looked up sharply, curious more than insulted. "I don't want you to go, you idiot. I was pretending to want you to go because I thought that's what a good sister would do. As far as I am concerned, you can stay home with me until you take a gap year before college, and then we'll go to college together, and then we'll live next door to each other in matching apartments in some big, cool city together for the rest of our lives. That's what I want, but I didn't want to keep you from your dream, and your dream was Truegrove."

"Truegrove is very, very, very much *not* my dream."

"Then whose dream is it?" They both knew the

answer. "You have to tell them, Milo. Tonight." She wrapped him in a hug and pushed him inside.

They heard all the parents troop into the kitchen.

"What's on the menu, chef?" Mac's mom asked Milo as he walked back in the house.

"You'd have to ask him." Milo gestured to Mac, who was seriously stirring something in a frying pan. Carole exchanged glances with Em and Julia but didn't say anything. As Milo set the table, Mac called out to him, "Ready to plate?"

There was a general murmur from the parents' end of the table of "What's going on?" and "I don't know" and "Who are these kids?"

Avery came downstairs as Mac was placing hot plates of lobster linguine in front of each parent. "What's with this?" asked Avery.

"What's with your eye shadow?" Mac shot back with a smile. Avery'd forgotten that she still had fake eyelashes on and purple glitter eye shadow plastered under each eyebrow. She sat down and bit into one of the rolls that were steaming in the middle of the table.

"You two haven't done anything together without fighting since ever, so, um, what is happening?" Andrew asked.

"Glad you asked." Milo and Mac took a breath at the exact same time. "Turns out Mac likes to cook," Milo said. "I don't. So we're switching."

"Okay, I don't think we really needed a whole announcement—" said Avery.

"Shhh." Lina nudged her, whispering, "This is going to be good."

"Honey, why didn't you say anything?" Milo's moms said in unison but with very different tones.

"That's not the only thing we're switching," said Mac. "Milo doesn't want to go away for school. I do."

Mac couldn't look at his mom, who he was sure would be crying, so he looked at Milo's moms instead. Em was her usual unreadable self. Julia had her therapist face on—interested but neutral, staying calm so as not to scare the animals. Milo did Mac the favor of looking at Carole, who was, as expected, crying into a rainbow-colored bandana, but smiling too.

"You guys might want to, um, keep talking," said Avery.

"Right. Yes. Okay. Well, that's it, really," stumbled Milo, staring at his own plate.

"No, it's not. Mom, I hate school. You know this. But I love being on the water—"

"And nearly getting arrested on the water," Avery chimed in.

"Shh!" said Andrew. "Let him talk."

"And Sam told me about this semester school." He reached into his pocket and passed over the folded brochure, already wearing at the folds from how many times he'd opened it and closed it that day. He cleared his throat. "It's school on a boat. You learn just like you do at home, but you're also navigating and doing cleanups and working the boat. Mom, I love you. But I need to try this for a while. Can I try this?" His eyes went wide. He couldn't remember the last time he'd wanted something so much.

Carole said nothing as she pushed up from her chair and ran over to Mac's end of the table. She kissed him on his cheek a million times, tears mixing with her lip balm.

"Mom," Mac laughed, "can I?"

"Oh! I didn't say that part out loud? Yes. I'm not sure how we'll pay for it, but we'll figure it out. And I'm coming to visit you every weekend. I'll take my chances with the Coast Guard."

"Mom!" Mac said in fake horror.

"Fine, every other weekend."

"Mom!" Mac said in actual horror.

"We'll figure it out."

Mac smiled and reached one awkward arm around his mom for a hug. Milo glanced up to see if maybe Mom and Ma were coming to hug him too. If they were just as happy and relieved as Lina was and maybe he didn't need to say anything else. Instead, Mom had crossed her arms over her chest, which was never a good sign. The barbed wire tattoo that she always talked about getting erased but never did bulged across her biceps, and Milo figured that it was for moments like this, when the barbed wire seemed to cover her entire body, that she didn't erase it.

Ma was leaning forward, her best tell-me-more face on full display. Lina squeezed his hand under the table.

"Um. I know how proud you guys are of my scholarship to Truegrove. I know that finding a school that would let me take all those languages, play soccer, and probably send me to the best college ever is a big deal."

"That's an understatement," said Ma.

"Shh," said Mom.

"But I also know that you taught me to be honest and to be myself. And if I'm going to stop doing that now, just to make you both happy, then I'm not sure that I'm as smart as you think I am. It's not that I'm scared, or not *just* that I'm scared, and it's not that I'm ungrateful. I'm just not ready. I'm thirteen. I've had kind of a lot of adventures in my life already. I don't need a new one right now. Plus, until Lina's dream of having apartments next door to each other for the rest of our lives comes true, I don't want to miss out on my last years of twin cohabitation."

Lina squeezed again.

"Presumably, I'm going to be smart for the rest of my life. But I'm not going to live at home for the rest of my life. I'll go to a good college no matter what. I'll read a lot and learn new things no matter what, just like I have for the last thirteen years. But I want to do it with you." He didn't realize that he'd been staring at his shoes, but he looked up, finally, holding his breath.

"It's hard to argue with that, isn't it, babe?" Mom said to Ma, who didn't answer because she was trying to wipe a tear from her eye without anyone noticing.

"So I can stay?" Milo exhaled and smiled, trying to keep the tears stuck in the corners of his eyes.

"Forever," Ma said, her voice shaking a little.

"Forever," said Lina, resting her head on Milo's shoulder. "But we can't. Avery, we need to get to the Crown and Anchor *now*!"

♡

There were other shows in town that night—award-winning actors, dancers, musicians, and comedians filling every stage up and down Commercial Street. But judging by the anxious excitement filling up the Crown & Anchor, there was no hotter ticket than the Family Week Talent Show. From little kids tripping in their tap shoes to the tweens tripping in their first drag to the occasional singer who could bring the house down, it was an event not to be missed.

And Lina, Milo, Mac, and Avery never did. Milo and Mac wanted to sit on the stools at the bar, but Kevin and Andrew insisted, as they did every year, that they get as close to the front as possible.

"Oh, great, spit row," Mac groaned as they sat very front and very center.

"You don't love spending your evening getting spit upon by baby drag queens trying to perform original ballads?" asked Milo.

"Somebody split these two up," said Em. "Obviously them getting along only leads to terrible things." But Milo could hear the laugh in her voice, and it felt so good to stop worrying for the first time in months.

After seven lip syncs, two failed death drops, more than a few cringeworthy original ballads, and a surprisingly good dance routine by a set of triplets, the lights went down yet again. When they came back on, Avery stood in the middle of the stage, a spotlight shining down on her.

Well, not exactly on her—on her feathers, really. She had a gold-sequined headdress, which gave way to a gold bodysuit with red and yellow sequins shining like a million diamonds. She had studded her tights with rhinestones, and red and yellow flames chased up her legs from her boots. Her arms, outstretched, so still, so strong, had long gold feathers coming down like she was about to take flight. They too glimmered, shiny like knives. Milo and Mac grinned.

"This poem is called 'Just the Facts,' " Avery started.

Fact One: Nothing has been normal since December.

Who gets divorced on Christmas, anyway?

Fact Two: I wanted a mom when I was little. I loved my dads, so I blame Disney and Pixar and Netflix.

So here's to you, Morticia Addams and Lady Elaine and Mama Llama and Mummy Pig. And why doesn't anyone know Simba's mom's name? It's Sarabi. And why are the moms always dead in kids' movies? Because there's nothing worse than not having a mom. What else was I supposed to think?

Fact Three: Being the child of divorce comes with a superpower. My parents are now terrified of me. You're terrified that I'm angry (I am so angry), you're terrified that our family is over (it is), you're terrified that you've broken me (so am I). I'm terrified that I'm terrifying.

Fact Four: I've stolen fifty-one lipsticks since February just to see if you'd notice. You haven't.

Fact Five: The prettiest, best girl I know writes a good letter. I can't answer it. Can you ever fall in love if your heart starts off broken before you even begin?

Fact Six: Family Week when your family has fallen apart is awkward.

Fact Seven: Every night before I fall asleep, I curse that five-year-old who wanted to be like everyone else with a Morticia of her very own. I should have been more specific.

Fact Eight: Weird feels normal and normal feels weird and nothing feels good and I just want to feel good again. My favorite thing in the world when I was little was falling asleep to the sound of a grown-ups' dinner party. Shrieks of laughter and trills of music floating through the walls, surrounding my bed, promising a future full of nights like these.

Now those memories don't sound like music, but like the screech of a wheel turning hard, a nail down a chalkboard, stop. Stop. Stop.

Fact Nine: I didn't know that missing and anger were such close cousins, but they live inside me now, never one without the other.

Fact Ten: When there's Family Week but no family, your arms might shake, you might cry, but that's when all the stuff they've been telling us for years proves true. Family is the family that we choose. But what do you do when they don't choose you?

"Thank you." Tears streamed off Avery's face, but her voice didn't crack, not once. She bowed, and the room exploded with applause from everyone—except her dads.

☆

When the show ended, Em, Julia, and Carole exchanged baffled looks. They knew better than to try to catch Kevin's and Andrew's eyes.

"We'll see you all back at the house," Julia said calmly as she led the rest of the crew out the door.

When Avery came out from backstage, Kevin said, "First things first." And he hugged her tight and pulled Andrew into the hug too.

"Now," he said, "let's take a walk."

They walked down Commercial Street for what felt like an eternity. They let the noise of the crowds make up for their silence: drag queens shouting for customers to come to their shows, ice cream purveyors with free samples, missed connections reconnecting across the street. It provided a buffer for the conversation that they all knew was coming but had no idea how to start.

Once they hit the West End, it was really quiet, only the occasional noise from a backyard party floating over them.

"Where are we going? I've never been down this far." But neither of her fathers answered her. The lights of a nearby hotel lit up the beach, and the waves lapped quietly at its shore. Huge rocks made up a jetty that seemed to stretch straight out to the moon on the horizon.

"Come on," Kevin said as he led them down to the water.

"Are you going to drown me?"

"Yeah, kid," said Papa, "this is it for you. . . . No, it's just beautiful, so sit here and take in some of the beauty, okay?"

The moon was huge over the water, lighting their way. Water licked at the rocks, and Avery sat at the edge and dipped her fingers into the cold black waves.

"Avery," Daddy said, but his voice caught.

"I know," she said. "I'm sorry. I know you guys must be embarrassed. I didn't do it to hurt you, I just—"

"Shhh," Papa said. "Let him finish."

Daddy smiled.

"Avery," he tried again. "I am so proud of you." Avery looked up. "That was so brave, and beautiful. You are such a good writer, and you know what to do with your words. You know how to use them to get your voice out when no one is listening."

"Really?"

"Really."

"You have a gift, kid," said Papa. "And tonight you learned how to use it. It's a call, it's a freaking shofar, it's a fire. When maybe your parents are a little distracted, a little busy paying attention to their own dramas and heartaches, you use your voice like the beautiful bell that it is: *Here's the truth, you jerks who I love, listen up.*"

Avery smiled. "I thought you would be mad."

"At myself, maybe," said Daddy. "Not at you."

"I think I can speak for both of us," Papa said, "when I say that we aren't mad at you at all. Your poem did what good art does—it made us look closely and feel deeply."

"I am sorry," said Daddy, looking toward the big moon. "Sorrier than I can say. To both of you."

"I know," said Avery.

"But you don't need sorry, do you?" said Daddy.

Avery shook her head.

"You need dads."

Avery nodded. "But you're about to be too busy being someone else's dad. You're already too busy."

"Avery." Daddy took a deep breath. "I am sorry you have to learn this now. I am sorry I am making you learn so many things. But one of the things you're going to learn is that love can't be quantified or counted. Just because I give some to someone else, that doesn't mean there's less left for you." Avery didn't say anything, but she didn't snap at him either. "It's not that there is room for you in my life, Avery, it's that you *are* my life. You and Papa both are. Even when I've made a huge, huge mess of things. Even when it's going to look different than it has. I know you might not be ready to be a big sister, but you're always my daughter, no matter what."

"You know," Papa said, "we've never done this before. None of us. So, we're not that good at it. But I think we can get better. We'll try some counseling when we get home, the three of us."

"Isn't family therapy for families?" she asked, sounding sarcastic and also meaning every word.

"Avery Angela Goldstein-Brown, we are a family." Daddy's voice was louder than he meant it to be. "I think that after all of these years at Family Week, you might have taken the wrong message. Family isn't like a Big Mac—always the same no matter what. Family isn't the place where things never change. Life is change, even when we don't want it to be. Family is the place where, no matter what else changes, you love each other. And that doesn't change. Whoever you are, whoever you become, we will always love you. And you, even when you wish you didn't, you will love us. And I, even though our relationship looks different than it did, will always love Papa and his bad jokes and his big heart." Daddy squeezed Papa's hand.

"And I'll always love Daddy and his good food and his terrible taste in women."

Daddy laughed, and so did Papa, which made Avery laugh. A week ago, that joke wouldn't have been funny, which made it even funnier. They sat under the moon, laughing until their sides hurt, until they didn't even know why they were laughing.

"Now, about those lipsticks," said Papa.

"What shades are we talking? Berry, cherry, mauve?"

"Not the point, Kevin, not the point."

"Right. Of course. You're going to need to pay all the stores back. And I know you, and I know that I didn't raise a child with terrible taste. Let's say each lipstick cost twenty dollars, I believe that'll be . . . one thousand twenty dollars, pal."

"Hmmm. I might not be ready to be a big sister, but how much does babysitting pay these days?" asked Avery, and her dads' arms linked together as they held her.

Saturday

♡

GOODBYES WERE AWKWARD. WHEN LINA WAS little, she would wake up on the last day of Family Week and hide in the car until it was time to go, refusing to say goodbye to anyone. But today, for the first time since New Year's Eve, she woke up and she couldn't feel the tight, whirring pit of her stomach. Maybe the pit hadn't just come from her love for Avery; maybe it was also her worry about losing Milo to Truegrove. Just like Avery said about anger and sadness, love and worry seemed to be close cousins too.

But only love was here this morning. She bounded over to Milo's bed to shower him in it.

"WAKE UP!" she said, putting him gently in a headlock.

"What in the name of every gay holy thing is happening?" Milo moaned.

"You're staying!" she said, gripping him tighter.

"Here in Provincetown? No, we all check out today."

"You know what I mean, loser."

"Maybe I should reconsider," he joked, wiggling free. "Jokes aside, though . . . it's not for you."

"What?"

"I'm not staying for you. I'm staying for me. You're just a perk."

"Wow, I'm touched."

"Maybe you should have eaten me in the womb when you had a chance."

"A daily regret." Lina shoved him off the bed.

When he came up, he had a more serious face on and a sheaf of papers in his hand. "Here."

She pored over the familiar pages, all the drawings she had spent hours making of Milo, Tock, and the Humbug. Words filled the pages now: Hunanese first, then Spanish, French, Portuguese, Greek, English, Hebrew, and finally a page of what looked like sound waves with the occasional consonant.

"Wait, is this—"

"Fishbish."

"I didn't know you still remembered it."

"I don't think you ever forget your first language." Lina smiled Milo's favorite smile, the big one that seemed like it was going to break her face in half. Mac and Avery weren't wrong about twin language, but they didn't know about Fishbish. It had started as a series of squeaks and squeals when they were six months old, adding a few sounds here and there as they grew. The story went that when they were one, a stranger stopped Ma and Mom in the grocery store and did all the usual exclaiming over twins, stopping just short of the inappropriate questions about uteruses and sperm that most people didn't have to answer when picking out bagels.

"Do they have their own language?" she'd asked.

"I think they do," said Mom.

"I wish I knew what it was!" joked Ma.

Just then, Milo exclaimed "FISH!" at the top of his lungs.

"BISH!" squawked Lina.

"Guess they named it!" said the stranger. "Good luck learning Fishbish!"

Even as they had grown, adding words (or in Milo's case adding languages), Fishbish still came in handy. A short, sharp note could get Lina to pass the mashed potatoes at dinner; a siren-like shout could always find Milo in a crowd.

"You drew the sounds."

"I did."

"I love it," Lina said, holding the pages to her chest.

"I'm sorry it took me so long." Milo put his head on Lina's shoulder.

Avery poked her head into their room. "Hey, twinners, you better get downstairs. If you make me miss the best pastries on the planet, I'll never forgive either of you!"

Downstairs, everyone was waiting. "It's almost like you people don't like the rebandaids or whatever," Em said as Avery, Milo, and Lina came into the kitchen.

"Rebandaids?"

"You know, the toasty things with the sugar from the place."

"Rabanadas?" said Milo, blushing slightly at his perfectly uvular trill, the rolling *r* that started at the back of his throat and came out as air, the long *a*'s floating through his nose. He hated it when his moms made him trot out his language skills at restaurants or at airports, hated the idea that he might seem pretentious or condescending. But he hated the word "rebandaids" more.

"Yeah, like I said."

Milo rolled his eyes, and they walked out the door to the Portuguese Bakery.

The breeze tasted like sunshine, and it blew the pride flags sweetly as they walked down Commercial.

Everything had a different sparkle to it on the last Saturday of Family Week. They stood on the bakery's brick steps and waited in the long line, inhaling the sugar-and-cinnamon air. When they got to the front, Milo watched in horror as Em opened her mouth to say "Nine rebandai—"

"Nove rabanadas, por favor," he interrupted. Without looking up, the baker handed Milo a bag heavy with grease and heat. When he gave him his change, he graced Milo with a quick smile and an "Até logo, menino." Milo glowed.

As they all ate their rabanadas out on MacMillan Pier, Julia cleared her throat. "So, are we going to talk about it?"

Kevin and Andrew looked at each other.

"Yes," they said in unison.

"We're sorry we didn't tell you earlier," said Kevin.

"We wanted one last Family Week, and we were worried that if we brought the divorce with us, it would ruin it for everyone."

"Turns out," said Kevin, putting his hand on Avery's shoulder, "those just aren't the facts."

"So," said Em, "there's a baby?"

"There is," said Kevin. "And, um, a lady."

"So I gathered." Em was quiet for a few minutes. All the adults were. "Well," she said, "I guess we're going to need a bigger house."

Kevin and Andrew smiled. "Thanks, Em."

"No more of this 'last Family Week' nonsense," said Carole. "Queer people know better than anyone what it means to make a family. This is our family. This is our week. That doesn't change just because we do."

"Hear, hear," said Andrew, raising a bottle of orange juice.

"To family," said Kevin through tears.

"You know what this trip is missing?" Lina asked the group. "Sweatshirts."

Everyone groaned.

"Come on, you know you want to. When was the last time we did it, three years ago? I'm not too cool to rock a matching sweatshirt, and I promise that none of you are too cool to match me either. We don't know what this year holds, people—look at what this week held! At the very least, a sweatshirt is in order."

Until the kids were ten, every year they would all end the week by going into the silliest souvenir shop they could find, and one family would pick out matching sweatshirts for the whole crew. "I Love My Gay Dads/Moms/Mom/Kid" shirts for everyone, or "Nobody Knows I'm a Lesbian" shirts for everyone. The year Kevin and Andrew got their way, it was very elegant, understated white sweatshirts with a simple black "Ptown" printed across the chest. The next year, Carole got them back with tie-dyed shirts with rainbow whales on them. But the summer they turned eleven, Mac refused to wear his, Milo and Lina couldn't agree on which ones to get, Carole got stressed about missing her ferry, and everyone went home without a sweatshirt. They hadn't tried again since.

Lina decided they needed to try something new. Everyone followed her to Womencrafts—the store with the 15-percent-off lesbian discount and an excellent selection of souvenirs. She grabbed Avery by the hand.

"We're picking. You all can wait here," she ordered with a smile. The grown-ups dispersed for coffee, and Milo and Mac sat together on the bench.

"Good luck at sea," Milo said.

"Good luck at home."

"I'm sorry—"

"I am too," said Mac. And they sat in happy silence for the first time since before the War of the Beluga when they were eight.

"Okay, check 'em out," Lina said, modeling her sweatshirt and placing one in everyone's hand. They were in all different colors: rainbow tie-dye for Carole, red for Milo and Em, bright pink for Avery and Julia, navy for Mac, purple for Lina, black for Kevin and Andrew, the word "Family" right across the front of each of them. "You don't have to say it. I know they're perfect."

Even Mac slipped his on. "They kind of are," he admitted.

"Okay, people. Back to the house. There's packing to do," said Em. And so they walked down the middle of the street, soaking up their last walk in a land where the pedestrians made all the rules. They were sweating slightly in the sun, but everyone wore their sweatshirt all the way home.

♡

As soon as they opened the door, Em and Kevin started barking orders at everyone. Julia and Carole went to empty out the fridge, trash, and recycling. Andrew was off to clean the grill.

Em yelled, "Kids, don't make me tell you again—"

"We know, we know, pack quickly and don't lose anything."

"All right, then. Kevin, you dust. I'll vacuum." The house felt full of energy—whirring and whooshing and cleaning and zipping and folding. Lina sat on her bed.

"Oh, so you *want* your mother to kill you?" Avery asked, noticing Lina's clothes all over the floor and Milo's perfectly packed suitcases sitting ready in the corner.

"Come sit."

"Oh, even better, you want her to kill me."

"Ha ha. No, I'm just . . . I'm not ready to go yet." The week had been crazy, and long, and short, all at the same time. There was something magic to a place that could change your life in seven days, squeeze the truth out of everyone, and leave you with a sweatshirt to show for it.

"I know the feeling."

"How was it last night with your dads?"

"I thought they would be mad, but no. They know they messed up. They want us all to go to counseling when we get home."

"Like to get back together?" Lina sounded hopeful.

"No, like to figure out how this version of together might work. I don't know. We'll see, I guess." In her own way, in a new way, Avery sounded hopeful too. They were silent for a moment. Their hands sitting so close to each other, it was like they could hear their pinkies breathing.

"Did you mean it?" Lina asked.

"Mean what?"

"You know."

"Prettiest and best?"

Lina nodded, the words staying stuck in her throat. Avery put her hand under Lina's chin, making her look her directly in the eyes.

"I did. I do. And I know that I'm too broken to do this

right now. But hey, they say time heals all wounds, right? There's always next year." Their pinkies curled around each other. Lina smiled her huge Lina smile, *Next year next year next year* ringing in her head.

"LINA, DANG IT, I SAID PACK!" Em shouted from downstairs.

"How does she always know?"

"Why do you never pack?" Avery countered.

Mac and Milo came in to see the mess.

"Are you people just going to stand there and stare?" Avery asked.

"At first," said Mac. "Then we're going to help. Milo, hold this bag." He passed Lina's black duffel to Milo. "Lina, you go get your toiletries. Avery, you pick up anything off the floor that doesn't seem like toxic waste."

"Aye, aye, captain," they all said in unison, and laughed. Three minutes later, Lina was carrying her bag downstairs, tossing Em a *Did you doubt me?* glance as she tossed her duffel into the trunk of their car.

"Well, I guess that's it," said Andrew, coming in from the yard.

"I don't think so," said Avery. "There's one more thing. Who's got a sock?"

Mac raised his hand.

"Give one to me, Goober. And get in the ring." Milo and Lina moved the coffee table and the sofa out of the way before she could even ask.

"You're kidding," Mac said.

"I am not."

"You're on."

"In the words of your mother, no more of this 'last Family Week' nonsense, you hear me?" They grinned at each other, and Avery slipped Mac's sock on. "Your sock is gross."

"Then let me take it off for you," he said with an evil laugh. They circled one another slowly, each waiting for the other to make the first move. Mac dove at her ankle.

"Oh no you don't." Avery tumbled out of the way, going onto her knees to protect her sock, and tried to grab at Mac's. They were both red-faced and laughing. Finally, Avery performed her signature move, knocking

Mac down, sitting on his stomach, and grabbing his sock off his foot. She waved it like a flag.

"Who's next?"

Milo was up. Round and round they went, and with each win, Avery made the loser swear that they would attend Family Week the following year and stop with the nonsense. She swiftly beat Carole, Lina, and Julia. Em gave her a run for her money, her college rugby moves providing some nice dodges and formidable pummeling tactics, but ultimately she nearly threw out her back, and Avery took her moment of weakness to swipe her sock literally right out from under her.

"Okay, Avery," Andrew said, kicking off his shoes and tossing one of his socks to Kevin, who slipped off his sandals. "What do you say to two against one?"

Avery smiled. "I say bring it on, gents." And so Daddy and Papa circled in on Avery, swiping at her feet. She tried to jump onto Papa's back, but Daddy tickled her right on the side of her neck, and she fell off. Papa grabbed her hands while Daddy grabbed her sock.

"So," they said, "what are we doing next summer?"

"Coming to Family Week," Avery said, smiling through her defeat.

"And what else?" asked Daddy.

"No more of this nonsense."

"And that goes for us too. We'll do better with our nonsense," Daddy said, giving Papa a hand to stand up.

"Absolutely."

"It's that time, everyone," said Julia sadly. "We've got to get out of here." Resigned, sweaty, sad, and happy, they all headed for the door.

Carole locked it behind them. There was a weird cacophony of goodbyes from the driveway as everyone made sure to hug everyone else before heading off. It would be a long trip home. But this time, Mac would stand at the very tip of the ferry, watching the horizon get closer and closer as the wind rushed straight through him. On the plane, he would fall asleep on Carole's shoulder, dreaming of dark, dark water and hot sun. Avery would convince Daddy and Papa to stop for fried scallops at the terrible tourist trap right after the bridge. And when Mom, Ma, Milo, and Lina finally got home (and yes, there would be some fuming about the traffic on the bridge), Milo would unpack his matching suitcases as Lina sat on his bed, just because she could. Just because there was time.

Acknowledgments

The thanks here are innumerable. I am grateful to the folks of Provincetown past and present who let little queer me wander down their streets and into their stores. I am grateful to the folks of Provincetown past and present who let me roll a baby carriage into small spaces and make space for my kid the same way they made space for me. I am grateful to my mother, Amy Bloom, for having the foresight (or I guess just the sight) to take me to Provincetown at ten years old and then every year after that. It was just one of your many smart moves to save my life. And to do more than that, to celebrate it. I am grateful to my brother and sister, my favorite drag show companions.

Many, many thanks to Molly Ker Hawn, agent extraordinaire, for her unshakable faith in my gay little books, for her excellent advice, and for her near clairvoyance. Marisa DiNovis, thank you for loving Provincetown and the *Family Week* crew as much as I do, for helping me every step of the way with that funny thing called "plot" and your deep knowledge of shark attacks and good ice cream.

And thank you, always and for everything, to my wife, Jasmine.

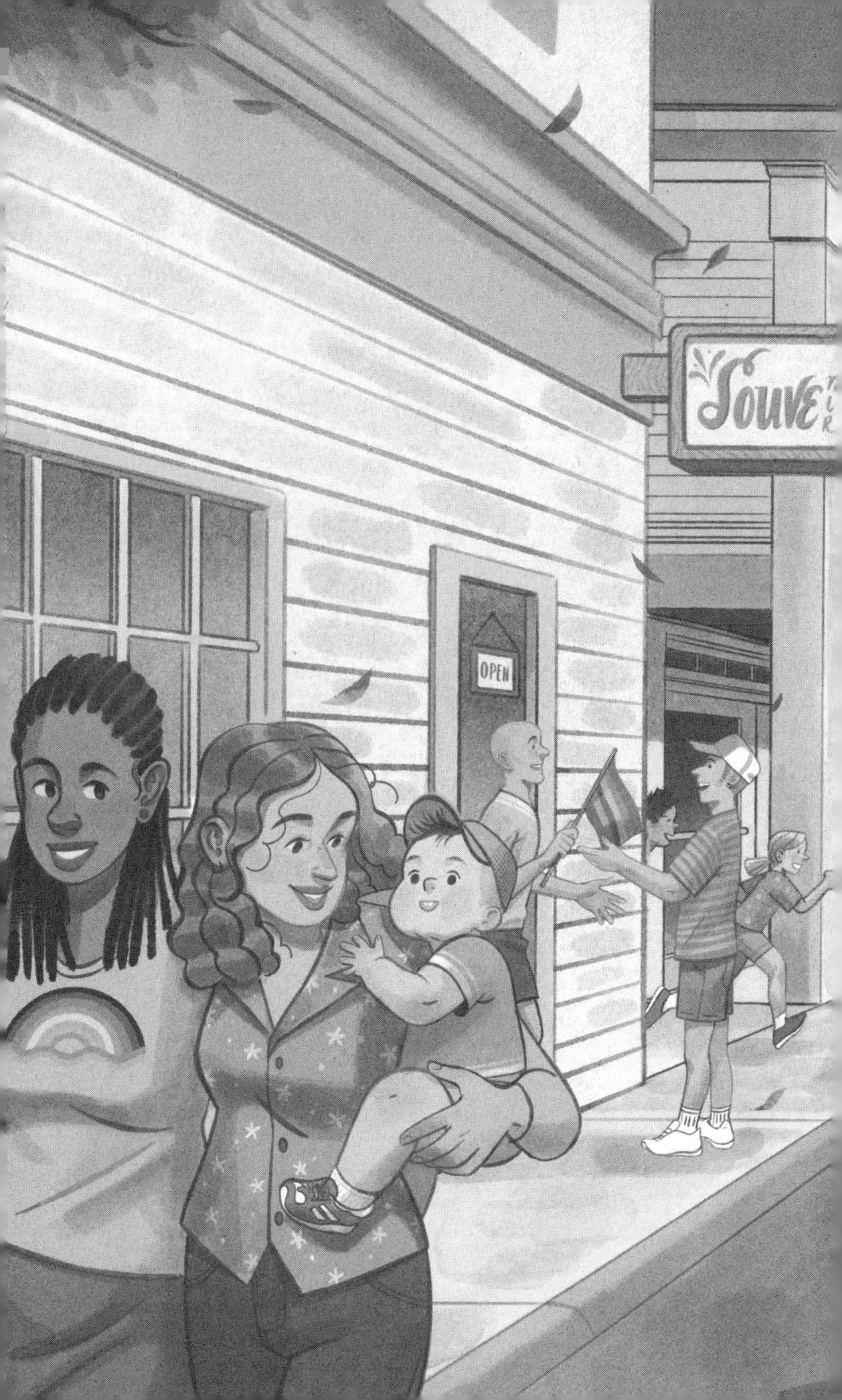
OPEN